HOWLING LOVE

HUNTER'S MOON RITUAL
BOOK ONE

M. SINCLAIR

LOST & BOUND PUBLISHING

The Union of Love & Madness

DESCRIPTION

Pain was the only constant in my life.

Love? Loyalty? Protection? Just whispers of hope I stopped listening to.

The Cold Moon Pack made sure of it—breaking me piece by piece, stripping away every part of who I was.

Until *they* crashed into my world.

Uninvited. Unapologetic. Impossible to stop.

Three dangerously possessive wolf shifters who I never expected to notice me at all.

One with golden eyes who watches me like I already belong to him.

One with a sharp tongue and a sunshine grin that hides a storm of violence.

And one tattooed in shadows, whose darkness calls to something fractured—and burning—inside me.

They didn't just see my broken parts. They claimed them as theirs.

But the world around us is unraveling. A war over shifter territories looms, alliances are crumbling, and the Cold Moon Pack's plans are darker than anyone imagined. The Hunter's Moon Ritual will grant them unimaginable strength—if they spill enough blood to take it.

Survival was never promised.

And the bond I share with my mates?

It wasn't a salvation.

It was a death sentence.

Howling Love is Book One in the *Hunter's Moon Ritual* trilogy—a dark, steamy, why-choose wolf-shifter romance packed with fated mates, primal tension, found family, and dangerous rituals.

Haunted by her past and bound to a future written in blood, Gracie never expected the possessive pull of three shifter mates—men who could be her only chance at freedom... or the ones who break her completely.

The Thornfell Registry is located at the end of Howling Love.

～

PROLOGUE

GRACIE

Ten years ago...

BRIGHT LIGHTS SWEPT across the icy ground of the pack compound as we stood frozen in place, metal handcuffs digging into my wrists. The iron was so cold it felt like fire, and every tiny movement sent a sharp sting through my arms. Blood dripped from my nose, little red drops falling onto the snow. It was the only thing I could focus on—anything to stop myself from looking at what was happening in front of me.

Had it really been only hours ago that I'd been sledding down the hill behind our farm with my brother? The sun had been bright, and even though the air was freezing, I'd felt warm. Happy. Safe.

But all of that had been torn away in seconds. I'd woken up to the sound of our front door being kicked in. Smoke filled the air, so thick I couldn't see or breathe. Everything happened too fast. I wished they'd left me there, in my bed. I wished they'd let me disappear with the rest of it. Because the person who dragged me out of that house wasn't an angel.

He was my new jailer.

Or *one* of them.

I'd heard the rumors—families taken in the middle of the night, homes burned, people disappearing. It was happening all over Thornfell. But my mom and dad always told me not to worry. They said we were safe.

I looked down to my left, where my dad's body lay in red snow. My mom knelt beside him, her cuffed hands resting on his chest, whimpering as she stared at his pale, still face. He had only asked for something to help me. That was all. He just wanted to help with the pain.

The burning on my side—the way I'd screamed when my new jailer shoved me into the wall of fire—it didn't matter anymore. I couldn't even feel it. All I felt was cold. Not the kind that comes from the snow or the wind, but the kind that numbs everything inside you.

The kind that didn't go away.

Even my wolf was silent. Too scared to make a sound. And me? I couldn't speak. I couldn't even reach out to comfort my mom.

On either side of us stood faces I recognized—neighbors from the village near our farm, people I'd seen at the market. But there were no kind smiles now. Just fear. Tear-streaked cheeks. Hollow stares. That alone told me what I didn't want to believe: we were never going home.

An armed guard stepped forward and shot a man from the village. Point-blank. The crack of the gun echoed off the metal walls of the compound, followed by the crunch of his body hitting the snow.

He didn't move again.

A voice cracked through the speakers overhead, the echo of it ringing painfully in my ears. "If you're willing to serve under Alpha Ivan, kneel."

My knees hit the ground before I even thought about it. Some part of me still wanted to live. Maybe not *wanted*, but needed. I couldn't die. Not yet. My mom was still alive. Owen was missing, and someone needed to find him now that Dad—

My brain refused to finish that thought. It just...stopped.

Shots rang out down the line. More bodies fell. The ones who hadn't kneeled.

"Yvelis is the only one who applauds your actions," the voice mocked. *The god of death.*

"From now on, your names do not matter. You will be assigned numbers as you integrate into the Cold Moon Pack. Any sign of loyalty to your former pack or community will result in your death. You will work until you've proven your loyalty.

"Your previous pack is gone. Your previous alpha dead."

Until now, I'd always thought Thornfell was beautiful. Harsh in the winter, but good. Safe. But tonight, with the moon missing from the sky, I could finally see the cracks. I could see the scars our jailers had carved into the land with their violence.

Even the ground felt different—like it didn't want them here. Like the snow itself had gone silent in grief.

As I stared at the cold metal wall, the voice over the speakers droned on, telling us about our future, about punishments, about what we'd have to become. But my mind was somewhere else.

I saw blue skies. Warm sun on golden wheat at harvest. My dad's cheerful singing in the kitchen. My mom crouching low, showing my brother how to hold a bow without shaking. For the first time since my father's body hit the ground, I felt the heat of tears sliding down my cheeks.

That world was gone. And in its place, only frigid darkness.

CHAPTER 1
GRACIE

THE WINDOWS SHOOK under the assault of the autumn wind as I stared uneasily at the dark gray clouds clustering above us. Thunder rumbled in the distance as I picked up the last potato in my bowl and started peeling.

The rain would be good for the water reservoirs, but during the last big storm, the mines had flooded. Six men were lost.

Not that it mattered to the Cold Moon Pack. Why worry about the lives of your laborers when you had so many? Especially if you could squeeze just a bit more work out of them before they drowned.

Disgust curdled in my stomach at the cruelty.

I hated this place.

Standing, I added the potatoes to the stock simmering on the stove. Alpha Ivan ate dinner at five on the dot every evening. If it sat out too long and grew cold—or if it was late—someone, namely me, would suffer. So my timing had to be perfect.

I wasn't exactly sure how I'd landed a position in the Alpha's house, and an easy one once I had overcome the learning curve of the cooking duties. But I wasn't one to look a gift horse in the mouth. Working here allowed me to stay invisible.

No one wanted to see the help, after all.

And it gave me the chance to make sure the leftover scraps were delivered to the children's barracks on the east side of the compound. Not exactly against the rules...but not encouraged either.

I didn't care. I was terrified of many things, but a punishment doled out for helping the children...that would be worth it.

Moving toward the cooler, I pulled out the prepared meat and brought it to the oven. While most of the kitchen sat cold and utilitarian—the metal surfaces and smell of boiled starches creating a cold shell—I'd managed to bring a little warmth into the room.

Many of the ceramic pots, pans, and baking dishes from the houses that had been raided nearby had been delivered to me for use. So the pale green casserole dish with the daisy pattern I used for the pot roast made me smile—just slightly.

I think those daisies were the only plants I'd seen

outside of vegetables in years. The land had revolted against the Cold Moon Pack, whether Ivan realized it or not. No vegetation would grow. No animals would stay alive. Everything had to be shipped in, because the place where we lived was dead. Starved of life, abandoned by Astaruun.

Even the people seemed like hollowed out husks.

For the past three years, I'd been sleeping in a servant barrack in the basement of the Alpha's house, alongside four others. But the years I'd spent in the outer barracks—watching my mother slowly fade, worn down by starvation and cold—had left a permanent mark on me.

I hadn't expected to survive long past her death. So when the transfer of job placement happened two years later, I took that small token of luck and clung to it with everything I had. I had no one in this world, not with both of my parents gone. But some small part of me—minuscule, really—still hoped Owen was alive. That one day, I'd find him.

So for now, I survived in the cold shadows of the formidable Cold Moon Pack, doing what I could to make each day a little more bearable for those around me.

Even if they didn't do the same.

"What are you doing?" Ravina's voice snapped. Out of the four other servants that lived in the Alpha's house, Ravina was the only one I interacted with often.

She was also the only one I had major problems with. More accurately, *she* had major problems with me.

Closing the oven and turning toward her, I offered a small, polite smile. "Putting everything in for dinner."

"You probably screwed it up, three-one-four," she growled, rolling her eyes and heading to the fridge.

At twenty-five, four years my senior, Ravina liked to throw her dominance around, always trying to pull a reaction from me. And using my old number like that —instead of the name I had earned when I moved into the Alpha's house—was meant to humiliate me. It wouldn't work, though. I wouldn't rise to the bait.

I knew exactly what happened when servants fought, and it ended with both of them dead.

"I left the salad to be done," I offered, wiping my hands on my apron. I didn't want to be enemies with Ravina, and I think in another life, we might have even been friends. Maybe.

Flicking her dark hair over her shoulder, she sat down at the table and began to chop vegetables, her pale fingers looking freshly bruised. I frowned as I instinctively moved closer. "Do you need something for your fingers—"

"Fuck. Off." Her brown eyes flashed with anger. "In fact, why don't you go get the bounty from the shrine? Get out of my face."

Inhaling sharply in frustration, I nodded and took

off my apron. It wasn't worth the argument. I wasn't particularly skilled at healing or medicine, but after having to treat my burns for so long after the raid, I'd picked up a few things. But unless it was really bad, Ravina wouldn't come to me. There had been one time when she'd been beaten within an inch of her life... but we never talked about it.

I had a good idea who had hurt her hand—the guard she was 'seeing' hurt her often. I had a feeling their relationship wasn't completely consensual, but we weren't close enough for that conversation.

Not that either of us could do anything to stop it.

Walking out of the kitchen and through the back door, I caught my reflection in the window.

I barely even recognized myself in the foggy surface, my steps slowing to a stop. Lifting my hand, I tugged my braid over my shoulder, the bright crimson color the only vibrancy I had left to me. My pale skin looked chalky, and my cheeks had hollowed from not eating enough. Even once-golden eyes looked dark now, as if the life had been drained out of me. It didn't help that I was only slightly over five feet, so in comparison to someone like Ravina, I practically disappeared.

It was as if I was a ghost. As if I had already died. I would argue that wasn't such a bad thing, given my current situation.

Pushing open the door and refusing to wallow in

my self-pity, I winced at the way my skin tugged on my left side. Ten years later, and I still felt the pull of my scars. From what I'd gathered, a third-degree burn like the one I suffered could have left me far worse off. So a burn scar that stretched from my armpit down to my hip—puckered pink skin that would never be smooth—was the least of my worries.

It had just hurt like hell while it healed.

The burn had fried my nerves so badly that, at first, only the outer edges of the skin hurt. But as it healed? While I was still forced to work in the camp, sorting through materials brought in from raids? There were days I cried silently while I worked. I'd tried to hide it from my mom because her hollow eyes told me she couldn't have handled seeing that.

"Afternoon, Gracie." The masculine voice made my stomach tighten uncomfortably, and I moved my gaze from the ground to Colyn. He was posted outside the Alpha's house on watch and was directly in my pathway to the shrine.

"Afternoon," I greeted, trying to shift my body as far from him as possible while slipping past on the stone pathway. When his hand wrapped around my arm and pulled me to a stop, I kept my face as neutral as possible, looking up at him.

"Where are you going?" he demanded. Colyn wasn't unattractive, but the malice I could feel rolling off him was enough to make my stomach revolt. I knew—or had heard—how he treated the women he 'favored' like Ravina, and I wanted absolutely nothing to do with him.

"The shrine. I need to grab the bounty for Alpha Ivan's dinner," I said, keeping my spine as straight as I could. If he made me late for Ivan's dinner, he'd face consequences, and I saw the disappointment flicker in his gaze as he released my arm and let me go. I practically scurried away, feeling a flicker of pride for managing not to shrink under his attention.

But damn, would I be thrilled if he never looked my way again.

The cracked concrete between the buildings would lead me directly to the shrine, so I kept my head down as I considered how much the compound had changed in the decade I'd been here. When Alpha Ivan had first staged his coup, the compound had been new, the central and largest one of several that existed in the territory. But the land had revolted against him, and while we were able to import many things, the lack of resources had taken its toll on the compound's state. From what I could tell, the Cold Moon Pack's territory was far from a shining example of success.

That was probably why he kept us isolated.

This territory was one of eight within the country of Thornfell. When I was growing up, it had flourished, blooming in every color imaginable across the vast landscape. I'd never traveled to the other territories, but I'd heard stories and seen pictures in school. Before the Cold Moon Pack stole our land, we'd lived like so many others under a ruling Alpha, but we had been able to trade, travel, and learn as we wished.

Now, the Cold Moon Pack had wrapped a chain-link fence with barbed wire around us. No one came in, and no one went out.

"Gracie, it's good to see you." Thalira said as I approached the shrine, where she stood in a dark navy robe tied at the waist. Alpha Ivan may not have believed in any sense of humanity or kindness, but he did seem to revere and fear the gods. Because of that, the shrine in the center of the compound was filled with flowers and fruit, all imported from other territories.

Thalira was the high priestess of our compound, and she, with her limited influence, managed to take care of those around her—discreetly, of course.

"You too," I offered softly, her warm brown eyes filling with affection. "Thank you, by the way." I didn't need to say for what. The leftover bounty the Alpha hadn't asked for last week had gone directly to the children's barracks.

"Come in," she said, motioning me out of the cold winds and into the warmth of the small building. Incense and the scent of fresh flowers filled my nose, and the warm glow of candles infused me with a sense of calm. My gaze took in the walls covered in tapestries, depicting images of the goddess Nyxarra. An altar stood at the front, symbols of the Mother of Shadows and Moonlight decorating the wooden surface.

In Thornfell, there were eight deities—*The Eight*—and it was said that each shifter felt a certain affinity toward one of them. Astaruun, the Creator—the one who gave life—had always held my attention more than the others. My parents had prayed to them as well. But now, that name wasn't mentioned. Nyxarra was the only god worshipped.

My gaze found a statue of her, her moonstone eyes seeming to watch me. A sense of awe and respect for the gods warred with what she represented to me. I looked back at Thalira as she spoke in a hushed whisper. "The goddess doesn't always approve of those that follow her," she said, as if sensing my thoughts. It was clear she knew the truth about how I felt—*I disliked Nyxarra because of Ivan's obsession with her.*

But maybe Thalira was right. Or maybe The Eight didn't exist at all.

"I doubt they even listen," I said honestly before offering her a small smile. "If you don't mind, I'm going to take the bounty back to the kitchen."

"Of course." She motioned for me to go, and I stepped forward to grab the basket in question, placing a blanket over it. Each week, the imported bounty of fruit was blessed and included in Alpha Ivan's meals throughout the week.

My mouth watered as I looked down at the basket, whispering a quiet goodbye to the priestess. My stomach grumbled, but I didn't allow myself the temptation to look under the blanket once more.

Tonight, like every night, I would get a bowl of gray mush and then go to sleep on a mattress thinner than my blanket.

It was just the way things were.

"Hurry, hurry," Ravina hissed, poking her head out the door as I reached the Alpha's house. I thrust the basket forward as I followed her back into the kitchen. The cart that would bring out his food was already set, and once she placed the basket on top to be presented to him, one of the other servants pushed it through the doors leading to Alpha Ivan's private dining room.

Ravina let out a huff and sat down, shaking her head. "That was way too fucking close, three-one-four. He's leaving tomorrow—this one had to be perfect."

Alpha Ivan was leaving? That was amazing news. Hopefully he was visiting one of the other compounds, or even another territory. The longer he was gone, the more rest it meant for me—and for others.

"Go get some rest, Ravina," I suggested softly. "I'll handle the cleanup."

Her face blanked at my unexpected kindness, then she let out a frustrated growl. For just a moment, I could feel her wolf rise up before she shoved it back down. She stormed off through the back door, and I watched her go with concern. Something was definitely wrong.

We may have been wolf shifters, but we had been taught that any show of our nature, whether in temperament or shifting, was explicitly forbidden. There was barely a shadow of my own wolf left. I knew she still existed, but the feeling of shifting? The connection, the union with the creature inside me? It would feel alien now. We weren't shifters anymore. We were bodies. Workers. Tools for the Cold Moon Pack.

The oddest thing about the Cold Moon Pack? It was relatively small. There were plenty of workers, but the actual pack members were a tight group of men at the top of the food chain—and the women they impregnated.

I would've called them *mates*, but no. That wasn't the case.

I knew that mates were real, a sacred gift from The Eight. A way to find your match, your equal. But not here. Not under Ivan's rule.

Here, women were bred. Used to produce pups. And then those pups were taken and placed into the children's barracks, where they were trained to become soldiers. I was beyond thankful I hadn't been propositioned yet.

The door to the dining room opened, and I realized I was still standing in place, deep in thought. My stomach twisted at the sight of Colyn stepping through.

Before I could say a word, he spoke—and what he said turned my blood to ice.

"Alpha Ivan would like to speak with you."

CHAPTER 2
GRACIE

MY STOMACH WAS COILED and tight with nerves as I walked down the hallway that once seemed short but now felt as though it was expanding. My heartbeat was going double-time, and sweat formed on the back of my neck. The walls felt like they were closing in on me, and while the house grew more luxurious the closer I got to the Alpha's living quarters, everything seemed to grow darker, more bleak. A cold chill ran across the floors as my fists tightened at my sides, the basic cotton dress I wore doing nothing to comfort me.

Why would Alpha Ivan want to talk to me?

When I reached the dark wood door of the private dining room, Colyn opened it, motioning me through. My footsteps echoed loudly as I stepped onto the polished wood floors, the noise making me wince. I kept my head down, as always, especially now that the shadows couldn't hide me. The scent of pot roast and the flickering of warm candles on the floor made the space feel decadent, luxurious. None of that mattered, though, because I knew—or could sense—three sets of eyes staring at me, drilling into my downturned face.

"Three-one-four—Gracie Holloway."

My head lifted of its own volition, shocked to hear my last name after a decade. The last time I'd heard it was when my parents introduced themselves to a vendor in the village market. *June and Cal Holloway.*

I didn't have time to savor the memory. Now that I was looking directly at him, my wolf recoiled with fear in the presence of the Alpha. My knees nearly buckled, my breathing turning ragged. If he saw my fear, he didn't react—nor did the other two men in the room.

"Is that right?" He arched his brow.

Alpha Ivan never struck the exact chord I would imagine, considering how he ran his compound. I didn't know how to describe it, but his polished appearance contrasted the state of the compound so much that it felt off to me. I knew how predatory this man could be, but he was able to hide behind his natural charisma. Even now, sitting across the room from me behind a polished wood table, he made quite the picture.

His silver-streaked black hair grazed the high

collar of his embroidered coat, his glowing amber eyes staring directly into my soul as I tried to find my voice.

"Yes." It was barely a whisper, but I knew he would hear it. The weight of their disdain pressed heavily against me, tainting the air. Not for anything I'd done, but for *what* I was. Always beneath them.

"Quiet, isn't she?" Beta Clint commented, his cold eyes glancing over me with clinical interest. I almost never saw the man, but when I did, his "mate" was usually by his side, looking like she was on the verge of tears.

"More than I can say for others," Enforcer Marek agreed.

"Submissive is good," Ivan stated in an evaluative tone. "Doesn't talk back. Appears clean. Young enough to still be able to have pups."

Bile rose in my throat. Why were they talking about me like this? I mean, I knew why—but why now?

"You think she's the one?" Clint asked.

The one for what?

I caught a perverse curiosity in Alpha Ivan's expression, as if he was thoroughly enjoying my confusion. I knew he wouldn't answer Clint—not yet.

He wanted me to stew in my fear a little longer.

"She's attractive enough," Marek agreed. "Has always shown loyalty, even when her mother died. She presents as fairly educated for coming to us at eleven."

"Can she read?" Alpha Ivan asked, then directed the question to me. "Can you, girl?"

"Yes." I managed to get out, a flash of anger filling my chest. It was unexpected, and I slammed it down before they could sense it. My wolf hated how we were being discussed, but this wasn't a situation I could survive unless I was silent. Though this was very possibly the end...especially if I was given to someone.

"She's a bit younger than expected," Alpha Ivan said. "I'm not sure how the dragon bastard would feel about that."

Dragons?

Within Thornfell, there were many different shifter types: dragons, wolves, bears, lions, foxes, and even prey shifters like rabbits. The hierarchy was based on shifting ability and strength, so most territories were run by dominant species like wolves or dragons.

That being said, I didn't know what dragons could have to do with this. I may not have had a lot of knowledge about the politics and territories of Thornfell since we were so isolated, but my understanding was that out of the seven other territories, only two were run by dragons—both of which were as far south and west as possible.

My knees began to tremble as I tried to breathe through my panic. I had no intention of interacting with dragons, especially when my wolf could barely rise in the presence of the wolf Alpha in front of me.

My eyes traced the patterns on the floor as they continued to discuss my state as if I were livestock. My hands tightened in my dress, equally terrified and furious. I could hear their words, but they were coded, never saying exactly what was going on.

My thoughts were broken when Alpha Ivan suddenly spoke directly to me, his voice smooth and relaxed. "Gracie, look at me."

Slowly, I looked up and held his gaze. Despite his easygoing demeanor, I instantly saw him clock my fear, and amusement filtered through his expression.

"Sit. Join us for dinner."

My eyes widened as I looked at the empty place setting in front of me, the round table made for four. With shaky hands, knowing that I couldn't disobey, I pulled back the chair and managed to ease myself into it as a plate was set in front of me. I stared at the food before looking back at Alpha Ivan. My pulse was thumping in my neck, and I could feel how sweaty my palms were as I waited on his next order—waited for *some* type of reasoning for my presence here. The suspense was agonizing at this point.

"Eat."

Slowly, feeling their eyes on me, I lifted the utensils and began to eat, bringing the food to my mouth. *I was going to throw up.* The first time I had real food in front of me in a decade, and I was going to throw all of it up.

"She even has decent table etiquette," Clint commented. The tremble in my hands turned into a tremor, my fork shaking in my hand like a leaf in the breeze, so much so that I worried I would drop it.

"Could be better, but with some cleaning up, it could work," Marek agreed.

The second bite had absolutely no flavor. My eyes stung with tears.

"There's no reason to be worried," Alpha Ivan stated easily. "You're about to get a promotion."

My fork clattered to the table. "A promotion?" I knew what that meant. Or at least I thought I knew what it meant.

"Yes. A promotion. As you know, the Harvest Moon Ritual will be happening soon."

How could I forget that the monthly display of blood and carnage was less than a week away? The blood ritual was meant to curry favor with the gods, specifically Nyxarra, in hopes of restoring the land, but they never yielded any results. Unless you counted the deaths of multiple workers.

The worst part? We were forced to watch. Sometimes to partake.

And if he was calling this a promotion...well, I knew my time was up. It meant I had been selected as one of the sacrifices gathered from across the territory.

"Before that though, I have to travel out of the territory for the TTC."

My brow furrowed. I recognized the abbreviation but couldn't for the life of me remember what exactly it stood for.

"She won't know what that is," Clint said. "It's the Thornfell Trade Conference."

"I want you to come with me," Alpha Ivan said.

"You want me to come with you to the Thornfell Trade Conference?"

"Like a parrot," Marek mused.

"Yes." Alpha Ivan nodded, seeming to find amusement at my surprise. "It will be counted toward what you owe to the Cold Moon Pack."

How could I possibly owe them anything else? I'd already given so much of my life to them.

Also, why wasn't one of his mates going with him? He already had two...

Unless...no. I wouldn't consider that. There had been no rumor he was looking to take another. I would rather sell myself to another member of the Cold Moon Pack than be Alpha Ivan's mate. Behind the civilized façade he was a master manipulator and a cruel master.

"Will that be a problem?"

"Of course not," I whispered.

"Good. It's settled. You may return to your quarters for the night. We'll leave in the morning."

I stood immediately and offered a small nod of understanding. Turning toward the door, I quickly slipped through, my eyes stinging with tears as I heard them chuckle at my fast retreat.

Colyn stood outside the door, giving me a dismissive glance as I moved past him. Thank The Eight he didn't try to stop me. I couldn't handle that, not after what just happened. My steps were quick as I made my way down to my barracks, the luxury of the living quarters upstairs quickly turning stark and utilitarian. I felt lucky to find it empty as I went to sit on my bed.

A promotion? This hardly felt like a promotion.

After several long minutes of calming my heartbeat, I slid off my shoes and made my way across the cement floor to the bathroom. Closing the curtain that served as a door, I slipped off my dress and undergarments before turning on the shower. The cold water hit my skin, and my eyes closed in relief as I let it wash over me. The temperature made me shiver, but my skin felt hot from the rush of horrifying emotions, so I accepted it willingly.

When I was done, I wrapped a threadbare towel around me before going to the sink. My stomach felt unsettled, and when I looked into the mirror, I could see the trepidation in my eyes. My face was drawn and exhausted, my eyes red with the tears I was trying to hold back, my lips blue from the cold shower.

Drying off my body, I let my eyes wander over the

scars that made the left side of my torso look like something out of a horror story. I ran my fingers over them, disappointed in myself. I shouldn't have viewed them that way. If anything, they were a sign of strength. If I could survive burns that bad and still heal, maybe I could survive what was ahead.

No. I *had* to survive what was ahead. I hadn't made it this far for nothing—no matter what tomorrow would bring.

CHAPTER 3
GRACIE

So *THIS WAS* where Alpha Ivan's mates lived.

It was a ten-thousand-foot leap compared to what most of us dealt with. For one, there was a radiator on the left side of the room along with a fireplace, the room warmed against the chill outside. Two large queen-size beds positioned on either side of the room sat covered with plush blankets and pillows, and a private bathroom was attached to the suite to my left. While Alpha Ivan's mates were mostly put away and ignored—so much so that I'd never even passed their quarters until now—he at least provided them basic comforts.

Serelina sat in the corner alone, knitting quietly. She was the first mate he'd taken and was pregnant with his seventh pup. I had no idea where her children were, or if she was even allowed to see them, but she seemed out of it, as if she wasn't truly present in the room with the rest of us.

Vianne, his second mate, was pregnant with her first child. She was only a few years older than me and was very vocal about being relieved she wasn't the one going to the TTC.

"I feel bad you have to go," Vianne said, "but honestly, I'll be glad for the break while he's gone. I shouldn't say that, but...I need rest."

That statement was upsetting for many, *many* reasons.

"If you just stay quiet and follow orders, it should pass by quickly. Plus, you get to see some new places, so that's good, right?"

"I suppose," I murmured, looking down at the dress I'd been placed in. And *placed in* was the right term—from the time that I'd woken up, I'd been in a process of transformation.

Vianne had been helping me get ready from the moment I'd woken up, transforming me from a ghost in a threadbare dress to a puppet draped in silk. She'd directed me to bathe in her tub, letting me wash the grime from my skin and nails, as well as shampoo and condition my hair. The last time I had seen any products like that—including a razor—had been back before the raids. Soap had been deemed essential alongside toothpaste, but nothing else. To say I relished in the bath, despite my anxiety, was an understatement.

I'd stayed still as Vianne and Serelina styled my hair, twisting it into neat braids and weaving them in an updo that felt far more elegant than anything I deserved. As they'd brushed my hair, my eyes had glazed over with a memory of the last time my mom had done the same in the cold barracks. How she'd whispered that the color of my hair—of her hair—had been passed on through generations of women in our family. The same was true for my father's side and my gold eyes, which seemed too bright for someone who felt so hollow right now.

Throughout that time, Vianne had explained a few things about the travel process and told me to expect some modern technology I'd yet to be exposed to. I'd thought she was joking—after all, before the raids, our family had owned a TV! But when she went into detail about phones, tablets, and smartwatches, I became overwhelmed and started to zone out. I would have no need to know about that stuff anyway.

The only comment Serelina made was that I needed to make sure to smile a lot—which, considering I'd never seen her smile, was surprising.

Finally, after I'd been rid of any remnant of who I was on a day-to-day basis, I was put into an outfit that felt heavy, like weighted chains. It shouldn't have. It was beautiful. The coat-dress was stiff, the stormy gray fabric buttoned all the way to my throat. It was the most durable and luxurious thing I had ever worn, but the silver embroidery around my wrists and at my feet where the garment brushed my ankles felt like shackles. Even my boots felt like armor. I knew I was traveling, but it was beginning to feel more like a prison transfer.

Or like I was being arranged like a vase of flowers to be put on display. I didn't often feel a sense of independence in my circumstances anyway, but right now it felt like my autonomy had truly been taken from me. Spending the morning in such a luxurious setting should have been a treat, but it had been more disturbing than anything else.

When the bedroom door opened, I was only half-surprised to see Ravina there. She held a bag that she dropped in front of me, eyeing me with distaste. "Where the hell are you going looking like that?"

"She's going to the Thornfell Trade Conference," Vianne explained. "With Alpha Ivan."

"I'm guessing you aren't coming back, then. I was just ordered to pack up all of your things," Ravina scoffed. Then her brow twitched, dipping slightly in confusion. .

Shock filtered through me. "What? What are you talking about?"

"I thought it was weird too," she admitted, motioning down at the bag. "I...I packed up everything

I could find of yours, including that little collection of jewelry you keep under your pillow."

My eyes stung as I offered her a small smile. I didn't think she'd known about that. "Thank you. That's from my mother."

"Whatever." She shrugged, tilting her chin up. "More room for me in the barracks if you're gone."

Except I could still see the concern she'd shown only moments before, and I didn't fully know what to make of that.

"I don't understand what's going on." I looked back at Vianne. "Why would I need all my stuff? Am I not coming back?"

Vianne frowned. "He didn't mention that—although he doesn't tell me much to begin with." Serelina looked up and shrugged. She didn't know either.

"I can answer that." Thalira stated as she stepped inside, carrying a small pouch of herbs. I recognized the medicinal bag. "You're being used as a bargaining chip."

A bargaining chip. An object to *trade* at the Thornfell Trade Conference. I should have expected this, yet Alpha Ivan's plans continued to blindside me.

I watched her blankly as she handed me the pouch of herbs, motioning for me to tuck it into my coat. I did so robotically, a numb sense of confusion leaving me struggling to form words.

Finally, I managed.

"Bargaining for..."

"You'll be offered to the leader of another territory in exchange for access to their resources." Her words were tight and filled with sadness, but with a tilt of the head she offered, "It means you're getting out of here, Gracie."

Was I truly worth so little, that I wouldn't even be told I wasn't coming back? That I would just be given away? I shouldn't have been surprised, I knew that, but I still felt a strong sense of rejection. Not rejection from Alpha Ivan, but rejection as...a human? As a person. Was I truly just tradeable?

"Damn you," Ravina growled, motioning toward me in a frustrated jolt. "This is ridiculous. What value does she hold?"

I couldn't even argue with her question. I wanted to know the answer too.

"She's young and pretty," Serelina said simply, stopping her stitch. "They're going to offer her as a potential breeding option."

The "pups" comment from Alpha Ivan and his men suddenly made sense. So *that* was my worth. Somehow, I had known that I would eventually come to this place, that this would be the situation I would find myself in—whether it be in the Cold Moon Pack or elsewhere. I was just a breeding option. My chest fractured as my last bit of hope drained away.

And all that was left? An odd sense of...relief. I had no

family here. I had no friends, not really. Here there was only sadness and pain. I didn't know who they wanted to trade me to, but at this point, it couldn't get any worse —could it? After all, I had heard from Alpha Ivan himself that he was the most ruthless of the leaders. So maybe, despite the dark future that could lay ahead, it wouldn't be as bad as this. That was all I could ask for.

"Who?" Vianne asked after a drawn-out, heavy silence. "I can't imagine it's the Grimfur Skulk." I nearly shivered in disgust. That would be...*horrifying*.

"No, they're already allies," Thalira said. "From what I gather, it's most likely the Stark Flight in the South. They have animal products that we've been unable to import recently." There was an undertone to that statement that I didn't understand.

"Then he plans to trade you to Waylon Kane," Serelina hummed. "Dragon shifter. Very old, but kind. Well, as kind as a leader can be."

My wolf let out a vicious growl inside my head, making my temples pulse. She clearly did not like dragons, and I couldn't fathom what she was saying anyway. Me? Given to an Alpha? That didn't seem right.

But I wasn't about to question it. I looked to Ravina. "I know this is asking a lot, but if I don't come back, would you mind making sure any leftovers go to the children's barracks every day? Please?"

Ravina rolled her eyes and shook her head in annoyance. "Whatever—sure."

When a knock sounded on the door, a now familiar thread of energy cascaded into the room, making my body still. Alpha Ivan. His eyes went to his two mates, offering them a look I didn't understand, but *they* understood it. Serelina gave a subtle nod and went back to knitting as Vianne offered a tense, awkward smile.

"Alpha, it's wonderful to see you," she greeted happily, but her voice was pitched slightly wrong.

"We're departing." Alpha Ivan's expression was kind, but Vianne flinched as if she'd done something wrong.

"Of course," I murmured, immediately standing. Not only did I not want to upset Alpha Ivan, but I hoped that my obedience would ease some of the tension in the room. When I went to pick up my duffel bag, Ravina's words moved softly against my ears, so quietly I barely heard them.

"Careful, Gracie."

Gracie? I couldn't remember her ever calling me Gracie. When I met her gaze, authentic worry shone in her eyes. I gave her a miniscule nod. Despite our differences, I think she considered us friends, somehow. Or at least allies. I didn't know what had changed, or if anything had.

Unfortunately, I wouldn't be around to figure that out.

As I reached the door, I realized Alpha Ivan had waited for me. He motioned me forward, and I straightened, feeling his eyes on me as I walked down the hall, his steps like drums behind me. Did he do that on purpose? Make it so that I felt like I was on death row, being escorted to execution? The way the coat tightened around me, the stiff material shifting back and forth, made me feel as if I were a wrapped-up present, being delivered to wherever Alpha Ivan decided.

The silence turned overwhelming by the time I reached the bottom of the stairs, waiting so that I could follow Alpha Ivan's lead. He circled me in a predatory way, raising a hand to grab my chin. His chuckle was cruel as I flinched, his bruising grip making my eyes sting. It wouldn't have been the first time I'd been hit, and a slap was far less than what usually occurred—especially when working outside of the house.

"Don't look so worried, Gracie Holloway," Alpha Ivan said after his laughter quieted down. "Your life is about to change."

CHAPTER 4
GRACIE

THE LAST TIME I'd been inside a car was a decade ago when we'd been transferred from our farm to North-grove, our compound. Of course I'd seen them come and go through the gates, but as I pulled the seatbelt across my chest, I couldn't help but compare the cold, sterile military truck from that night to the luxurious SUV I now sat in. The leather smelled polished, and I tried to take a breath to calm myself before Alpha Ivan got into the car with me. The last thing I wanted was to be in a confined space with him.

I knew the act, if you could even call it that, would drop very soon. I could already feel it slipping in the way he spoke to his Beta and Enforcer outside of the car. There was a harshness to his tone, a calculating cruelty.

Adjusting my jacket, I put my hand into my pocket and felt the herb pouch Thalira had given me. Eyeing the three men outside, I quickly took it out and peered inside. A note sat folded alongside a vial, the parchment warm in my fingers as I gently flattened it out.

"Only use this if there's truly no path left. This will carry you back to The Eight."

Inhaling sharply, I watched as the note broke down into ash, falling through my fingers and back into the pouch—removing any evidence of its existence. The words were seared in my brain, though, and I swallowed nervously. What had Thalira predicted that would require such extreme measures? I eyed the vial, realizing what it was: poison.

Would I really need to use it? That terrified me more than the contents of the vial itself.

As I stuffed the pouch back into my pocket, the car door opened. I tried to school my expression, silently eyeing the silver trim on my coat.

"We'll meet you at the airport," Clint said before closing the door for Alpha Ivan.

The two of us sat in silence.

This was going to be a horrible car ride, especially if he continued to stare at me like that.

"I have some calls to make. I expect you to stay silent."

My gaze moved toward him, and I nodded in

understanding. His charming smile was gone as he looked down at his phone and dialed a number, the sleek metal device very different than the phones I remembered.

As his call began, I looked out the window, watching as the compound gates opened. I was leaving its walls for the first time in ten years, something that was impossible to fathom. Leaning forward, I watched the cold, dead landscape pass by minute after minute. It was early fall, but there was no vegetation. No longer did bright, vibrant orange and red maple leaves decorate the trees.

My expression must have been obvious, because Alpha Ivan's voice was hard and sudden, making me flinch. "The territory you remember doesn't exist."

Clearly.

"Why do you think that is?"

His question had panic tightening in my throat. I couldn't say the real answer, that The Eight had abandoned us and the land. It was a trick question, and if I answered it wrong, I'd get hit. Hard. That wasn't an assumption, either. I'd suffered at the hands of his pack for far less.

"I don't know," I answered softly.

"The vermin that lived here salted the land before our coup. Because of them, nothing grows." His answer had my wolf snarling. The sensation made my heart seize in surprise. My wolf had been silent for so long, but with what we'd gone through in the past twenty-four hours, something had ignited in her. In us.

And Alpha Ivan's answer? Ridiculous. I had lived on a farm my whole life, and this kind of destruction didn't come from salt alone. Not to mention that *I* was one of the vermin he referred to.

Luckily, I was saved by another phone call, and my gaze returned outdoors. An airplane—a jet, more specifically—sat waiting for us behind a chain link fence. I loathed the idea of flying. I had no reason to, but I'd never been on a plane in my life, even before the coup.

And I didn't want to start now.

Questions began to grow in my head, accumulating—amassing—as the silence itched beneath my skin. I needed to know...something. Before I could stop myself—before fear could drown the words—I spoke.

"Where are we going?"

Alpha Ivan stared at me with contempt, as if any spoken word from me, unless it was in direct response to his prompting, was an insult. Sinking back against the seat, I let the question hang rather than apologize. I didn't want to make it worse.

"I suppose you deserve to know," he said, hanging up his phone. "We're going to Central Thornfell. The TTC is being held in the Scarlet Sloth territory."

Bear shifters. My wolf didn't seem nearly as upset about that as she had about dragons, so that was a positive. Now I understood why we had to fly. Central Thornfell was a long way from the northeast corner of the country where we lived. At least a few hours, minimum.

The only hope I felt was in the significant fact that if I was truly being "left" or "given away," it would be far away from the Cold Moon Pack.

The car came to a stop, and Alpha Ivan motioned to the door with his head. "Out. Now."

I scurried out of the seat, straightening myself and keeping my gaze on the plane, avoiding eye contact with the gray-uniformed men around us. All men— except for one woman descending the jet stairs. Her once-over had me shrinking into myself.

"Alpha Ivan. Good morning for flying."

"Velina. I expect you have everything ready?" he asked sharply.

She nodded, then looked at me again, analyzing me with a hawkish gaze. "This is the one?"

"Yes. She'll need a debriefing before we land. Assume she knows nothing."

I hid my reaction by looking down at my heavy shoes, brow furrowing with annoyance. I'd been kept ignorant, I knew that, but I didn't like being reminded of it. I would have given anything to live in the larger world instead of clawing through each day just to survive.

I didn't even realize Alpha Ivan had moved past us and up the stairs until Velina's hand gripped my forearm, snapping my attention back to the present.

"If you want to survive this, girl, you'd better school those reactions. Now come."

VELINA'S WORDS had the desired effect—fear. An hour later, I was tucked away in the back of the jet, avoiding attention from the pack leaders. I could smell alcohol in the air and hear the sound of glasses clinking, as if they were celebrating. The gray uniforms had disappeared, replaced by dark, expensive suits with flashy watches and silver embroidery. They matched the luxurious nature of the jet perfectly, and I had to wonder: if Alpha Ivan liked this type of lifestyle, why was his compound so depressing?

Was it just to ensure we suffered, or was he putting on a show for the event we were going to? I had no idea, but considering the way Velina was trying to drill information into my head, I was going to assume the latter.

I'd already been berated for my inability to hide my reactions, and I couldn't even disagree with her— Ravina had told me it was a problem. I probably wouldn't be able to hide it, though. Not completely. I had learned how to get by in the compound by staying invisible, unnoticed in the shadows. But that wouldn't be an option here—so if keeping a blank face meant staying out of trouble, I would try.

Unsurprisingly, I'd also been told that I shouldn't speak unless I was asked a direct question. That I should smile, but not with teeth to ensure I didn't come off as too forward.

I was supposed to look peaceful and demure to serve as a useful representation of the Cold Moon Pack. Which was funny, since the Cold Moon Pack was none of those things.

"Your education is sufficient enough that you appear capable of a conversation," Velina said, opening a binder. I'd been told that Velina was some kind of assistant or emissary for the Alpha. I didn't know what that involved, but she seemed very thorough at her job. "You can read and write, which is more than some, but make sure you do not overstep or seem too curious. Questions don't come off the way you think they do."

I would've been insulted by how she was talking to me, but it made sense that someone in her position would view me no better than Alpha Ivan did, so I simply nodded. Now was not the time to argue that I was actually fairly smart. Not as smart as some, but intelligent enough to think for myself. Or at least I liked to think so.

"You do not have any education, though, on the politics of Thornfell or its leaders." She said it with the certainty of someone wholly aware of the walls Alpha Ivan had built around us, both physically and otherwise. The world could've burned down in the past decade, and we probably wouldn't have even realized it.

"Read the first one. Out loud."

She slid the binder my way, and I glanced over the chart of the leaders expected to attend the TTC.

"Alpha Graeme Sharp from the Grimfur Skulk, located south of us on the eastern coast of Thornfell."

"Fox shifters," Velina supplied, "known for trade in industrial supplies and seafood. Already considered an ally, so you should have no need to interact with him. However, if you are called upon to be useful, you should answer immediately."

I really didn't like the sound of that.

"Next one," she prodded, and I glanced down at a now-familiar name.

"Alpha Waylon Kane from the Stark Flight, located in Southern Thornfell."

"Dragon shifters, hopefully soon-to-be allies. They are known for trade in animal products—mainly livestock and meat. When you meet Waylon, you need to ensure you hold his attention. He should be the only

Alpha that you substantially interact with. Understand?"

I was thankful for the insight Thalira had provided me. Without it, her words would have been confusing. I nodded and continued reading without her having to prompt me. "Alpha Haiden Murphy from the Nightstar Flight, located in West Thornfell."

"Dragon shifters as well, led by a horrible woman who's extremely selfish. You should have no need to look her way, let alone interact with her."

Hmm. If Ivan didn't like her, the woman may actually be decent.

"What do they trade in?"

"Doesn't matter, but agriculture."

"Wouldn't that be important—"

Velina's look silenced me. What *I* thought the Cold Moon needed—what I thought at all—didn't matter. I moved on. "Alpha Chace Wall of the Blazefur Pride, located in Southwest Thornfell."

"Lion shifters. Trade in petroleum, namely crude oil products. We have a tenuous relationship with them."

We didn't seem to have many allies at all. I wasn't sure why that surprised me.

"Alpha Kaliyah Greene of the Scarlet Sloth, located in Midwest Thornfell."

"Bear shifters. Trade in crops, mainly wheat and grains. She's the host of the conference this year.

When you meet her, be respectful." Velina's expression told me she would expand no further on the woman.

"Alpha Lacey Harrison of the Bloodrose Sloth, located in the plains of Thornfell."

"Bear shifters as well. Trade in crops and agriculture," she said. "We have trade deals with them, but they aren't allies by any extent."

"The last one is Alpha Deegan Gentry of the Ironsun Pack, located in the central mountain range of Thornfell."

Loathing filled Velina's face. "Wolf shifters, unfortunately, who believe they have moral superiority over everyone because of the way they treat their territory's citizens. They trade in minerals and metals, but we will absolutely never have a trade agreement with them. In fact, if you're introduced to them, I suggest you don't even meet his gaze."

Because of the way they treat their territory's citizens. That sounded like they treated them with basic decency.

Velina snapped the book closed. "Will you be able to remember that, or do you need to take the book with you?"

"I can remember." It was the first scrap of knowledge I'd been given about the outside world in years. I held it tight, a lifeline tugging me past the steel bars that had locked me in for so long.

"You better hope you remember. Both of our lives

depend on this." Velina stood and returned to the front of the plane, leaving me in silence.

I wanted to hate the woman, but I recognized in her another person who was just trying to survive. I wasn't ready for this, but she was trying to ensure I at least made it through. And for that, I could be thankful.

I looked out the airplane window, something that wasn't as scary as I'd initially thought it'd be. The landscape thickened with green the further we got from Cold Moon Pack territory, replacing the concrete ashland with fullness and life. It was almost jarring to see so much green after this long.

Trapped in thoughts of what life would be like in a place that was so alive, I froze in panic when someone sat in the seat across from me.

Marek—Alpha Ivan's enforcer.

The man, who was nearly triple my size, invaded my space as he offered what I'm sure was meant to be a charming smile. To me it looked like he was leering. His gaze ran over my covered body as he leaned forward, placing a hand on my leg.

"Came over to check on our little present. All wrapped up and ready to be hand-delivered to Waylon. Excited?"

My body went cold at the casual objectification, the cruel way he found my future amusing. The way his hand was tightening on my thigh.

"I'm aware of what's going to happen." My voice was tight.

He chuckled, moving his hand back and forth and tilting his head in a predatory move.

"I heard that when dragons fuck, they shift—and if their mate isn't a dragon, they end up splitting them in half." Nausea filled my stomach as I gripped the armrest, causing him to bark out in laughter before sitting back in his seat.

"Gruesome, right? But I can make you a deal. How about we take a trip to the suite in the back of the plane and I give you a taste of fucking one of our own kind before you're discarded at the TTC?"

"No, thank you," I said quietly, trying to hide my revulsion. Unfortunately, my reaction made him angry, and he surged forward, clasping my jaw in a hard hold.

"You're right. I shouldn't have made it seem like an option. Into the back, now."

As he tugged me to my feet, I tried to twist away from him, my wolf rising up in defense. *My willing subservience to these people only went so far.* My thoughts raced, and I wanted to scream but instead a panicked sound escaped from the back of my throat, sharp and broken. The entire jet turned to look back at us.

Marek cursed as Alpha Ivan stood, his jaw clenched. Nothing was said. Nothing had to be said, because immediately, Marek threw my arm back. I stumbled and fell into the chair as the man stormed back to the front of the plane, and I was left breathing heavily, anxiety making my skin go clammy.

The relief that had initially burned through me now curdled in my gut. Needing Alpha Ivan's protection made the chains around me feel even tighter.

CHAPTER 5
GRACIE

THE CAR RIDE WAS SILENT, but this time it held a very different note. No longer was Alpha Ivan dismissive of me or indifferent about my actions. He broadcast his tension in the way he barked commands at people after we'd landed, in the way his fists clenched the steering wheel. I was doing everything in my power to stay as still as possible, not wanting to evoke his anger —though after the Marek incident I wasn't sure that was possible.

Somehow, the blame had also fallen on me.

Alpha Ivan didn't say that, but I could feel the disapproval.

"We'll be arriving right on time. I expect you to be prepared for the opening ceremonies. Do not disappoint me." I nodded immediately, not wanting to come off as disrespectful.

Even glancing out the window might be mistaken for defiance at this point—especially considering the way he was looking at the passing land in contempt. But contempt was the last thing that I felt. The beauty of our surroundings literally stole my breath as we drove into the city.

Nature blessed the land by integrating itself fluidly, welcoming the people that lived within the territory. There was an autumnal glow from the trees, and the crops were lush and ripe, moving with the cool wind. Fractured light from the clouds above moved across gardens nestled against classic brick houses. People moved in and out of them, walking alongside the country road we drove on, waving at the passing cars. Little did they know that inside sat a man who loathed them.

"Disgusting creatures," Clint observed, having been the only other individual allowed in the car with us. He was clearly trying to support Alpha Ivan's feelings on the situation. I bit down on my lip, trying to suppress a small smile. I shouldn't have felt satisfaction at their annoyance over this territory's beauty and success, but...

"The city should have less of them," Alpha Ivan muttered, as I moved my gaze further into the distance where, from the flat farmlands, rose a magnificent city. As we moved closer, the miles being eaten up by the speed we were driving at, I was taken off guard by the regal way the capital city was positioned like a crown jewel within the lush land around it.

As we reached the city limits, I ate up every single detail. There were domed copper roofs, turned green with time, and marble fountains. Bronze streetlights lined the streets, a flag featuring a black bear against a red crest standing proudly in greeting. Terraced townhomes with balconies covered in vines filled each block, and tiled pavilions featured market stands and shops. There was a rich history and authenticity to the city, but more than anything, there was a sense of peace.

The Scarlet Sloth region was everything the Cold Moon Pack was not.

"Here we are," Clint announced as we approached one of the domed buildings, the marble walls sparkling like diamonds as the afternoon sun broke through a cloud. I almost sighed appreciatively, but the moment was cut short when Alpha Ivan yanked me from the car. Once I found my footing, a familiar thread of fear coursed through me—especially when his hand closed around the back of my neck to keep me close.

"Walk," he ordered quietly, pasting a charming smile onto his face. Swallowing nervously, I kept my eyes down as his hand squeezed like a cuff, his large frame overshadowing mine to the point that I hoped I would disappear. Mostly because I could feel the eyes of others on us. I had to wonder what they thought. Did they think I was here willingly? That I was his mate? Or did they see me for the prisoner I truly was?

I'd always felt like I had a good gauge on the feeling of a room, and the moment we walked through a set of two-story doors and into a crowded foyer, I felt the temperature cool considerably. I kept my eyes on my feet, feeling shame for how I was being treated, knowing it was wrong.

Even more so, I wasn't ready to meet their eyes... not when I already knew what I'd find there. True distaste. It was clear to me, more than ever, that people *really* didn't like us. No words were needed to confirm what I could feel. Every step I took echoed my shame.

"Welcome, Alpha Ivan," a kind female voice said, causing me to look up.

I was caught off guard by the warm pair of maroon eyes that met mine. The woman in front of me was taller than myself, but slight in build, her golden figure wrapped in a loose-flowing red dress embroidered with brown and gold. Her brown and silver hair flowed over her shoulders and down to her waist like a veil. She was beautiful, practically glowing with life.

"Alpha Kaliyah," Alpha Ivan said stiffly. "Thank you for welcoming us to your city."

"Of course," she said pleasantly before looking at me. "And who is this? Your mate?"

"No," he said sharply, and relief filled my chest. I hoped others had heard that.

"Well, it's wonderful to meet you. I'm Kaliyah, and you are..."

I froze, unsure if I could or *should* answer, but Alpha Ivan let out a rumble of warning.

"Gracie," I managed. Alpha Kalilyah's brow furrowed just slightly, as if sensing something was wrong.

"Gracie. Lovely name. Well, we'll be doing the introduction ceremony soon, so please feel free to make your way to the line."

With that, Alpha Ivan abruptly departed the conversation and led me to possibly our only ally—Alpha Graeme Sharp. I'd seen photos of him once or twice; I'd even seen him from a distance at our compound while he'd visited. And every time that I saw him, I had a very visceral reaction—one of extreme revulsion.

His skeletal frame and his extreme height, brought together by the spider-like way he moved, set me on edge. I'd heard in the whispers of the servant barracks that he was Ivan's lapdog, and considering the way he seemed thrilled to see him, those rumors rang true. I'd also heard the man was completely absent of morals—that he would do *anything*. I couldn't fathom what that meant.

"Ivan. Wonderful to see you." He thrust a hand forward for Ivan to shake, his paper-white skin nearly transparent. His black, greasy hair hung past his shoulders in choppy sections, and he wore a brown velvet jacket with a gold fox on the crest. It was meant to showcase luxury, but something was off about the picture Graeme painted of himself. I just couldn't tell you what.

"Yes, unfortunately we had to spend far too much time looking at this place while driving," Ivan said, annoyed, and the two of them broke into conversation about their disdain for the territory. The jealousy was palpable.

"I hate her." A woman's voice drew my attention to where she stood with a scowl on her face, arms crossed and glaring at her assistant, who was attempting to calm her down. She wore a black jacket that reached down to her ankles, much like my own. But hers was adorned with a white bear on a rose-colored crest. This must be Lacey Harrison from the Bloodrose Sloths.

She was beautiful, with silver hair pulled away from her face, ruby earrings glinting from her ears as she continued to rant. "I can tell she thinks she's better than us—it's ridiculous."

"Of course, of course," the other woman said as Lacey's gaze snapped up to mine, sensing my attention. Her green eyes narrowed distastefully at me as she lowered her voice, and I drew my attention away, getting the message loud and clear.

She may have been talking poorly about someone else, but she didn't like us either.

"We'll be lining up to enter now!" announced a voice that echoed through the hall. Ivan's hand imprisoned me once more, marching us forward—but not too quickly—so we would be the last to enter. I had to assume that he viewed it as a statement of power, although I couldn't be sure. Before us was Graeme, but before him was a man who seemed amused by Ivan's appearance.

"And see here, I thought we were too lowly to expect a visit from the great Ivan," the man said bluntly. He paid Graeme zero mind—nor myself—as I tried to get a hold on the type of power he emitted. Bear shifters felt similar to wolf shifters to an extent, but this man's magic carried a different note.

"Alpha Chace. I would say it's good to see you, but it's not."

Ah, he was the lion shifter—that was why his magic felt different. The distinguished man had a commanding presence, accented by a natural confidence and charisma that made Ivan's attempt at a similar disposition a mere mockery. He wore a tailored black coat with accents of gold, and there was a warm gleam to his eye that Ivan didn't like, if his increasingly bruising grip was any indication.

"Don't be so bitter. Consider this a vacation—a paradise away from your cold, lifeless territory." His smile didn't do anything to soften his words, and the growl that broke from Ivan's chest made my eyes go wide. My wolf began to pace in my head as my heart thumped loudly in my ears. I hated that I had to be close to *any* of this, but I wanted to be far away from Ivan's wolf at all times. I'd once watched him rip out the throat of one of his commanders while shifted because he'd done something "wrong."

"Gentlemen, surely this isn't necessary, especially with a lady present," a woman said brightly. She appeared out of nowhere, a wave of magic slamming into me and causing my wolf to panic. *Dragon.*

I locked every muscle in place, hoping to become invisible. This had to be Haiden Murphy, her eyes meeting mine with a sparkle of knowledge. She was strikingly beautiful, her dark eyes like burning embers that sat under her strong brows.

Her complexion was a warm, sun-kissed amber, and her thick, dark hair was pulled away from her face and decorated with gold beads. She wore a deep emerald gown, cut to show off her athletic figure and the gold tattoos etched into her skin.

Everything about the woman exuded strength and purpose. She was completely unafraid to stand in the presence of these men, effortlessly dominating them.

"She doesn't care," Alpha Ivan said dismissively.

"And I'm shocked you didn't send your mate to handle things here, Alpha Haiden. Surely you have other, more important matters to handle."

"No. I don't." She turned to me, dismissing Alpha Ivan out of hand. "I've never seen you with Ivan before. What's your name?"

Alpha Ivan squeezed so hard I nearly gasped. The message was clear: do not answer.

Alpha Haiden received the message too.

"Right," she murmured, her eyes narrowing on Alpha Ivan. "It would be wise to treat your mate better around me, Ivan. You know how I feel about these things."

Then she was gone, and I took a deep breath as Alpha Ivan's grip relaxed. It felt like I had an axe hanging over my throat, the physical threat right within reach. If he wanted to, Alpha Ivan could snap my neck with his bare hands.

Alpha Chace turned back to the line, clearly done with Alphas Ivan and Graeme, but the man next to me was livid. I could practically hear his wolf growling. I really appreciated Haiden's concern, but it would only make things worse for me if she continued.

"Where is Waylon or Deegan?" Graeme's question was quiet but seemed to summon the first. I was surprised, because while I knew it was Waylon—the purple and gold dragon crest and the type of power coming off of him giving him away—he didn't appear nearly as old as I'd been told.

If I had to place him, I'd say he was in his mid-fifties. Then again, appearance didn't always correlate with age when it came to shifters. His angular face had scales running along the cheekbones, glinting green against his olive complexion, and his black hair was braided down his back, intertwined with a gold ribbon. The man had a dignified and elegant presence as he greeted our host before taking his place in line.

"Old man thinks he's better than everyone," Graeme grumbled, and my eyes widened. Surely he couldn't be older than Graeme...right? That didn't seem possible.

"He would be a good trading partner, though. Lots of experience," Alpha Ivan admitted. I pressed my lips together, keeping my reaction neutral, not wanting to give any indication of how I felt. While the idea of being sold off like livestock was repulsive, from what I could tell, Alpha Waylon seemed...okay. And okay was better than cruel. It was better than fear. I could survive "okay."

I was so trapped in thought that I didn't realize we had begun a processional into the hall where others were gathered—dignitaries and members of each territory who had come to the conference. I shifted nervously on my feet, but Alpha Ivan's hand tightened on my neck to stop me. So I switched to trying to take calm, deep breaths without him realizing it.

When it was our turn, I focused my gaze straight ahead to the table we would be sitting at. Eight large chairs with smaller ones to the right of each. As the table filled in and Alpha Ivan was announced—my name completely absent, unlike some of the other companions in attendance—I noted that there were four seats open. Two for us and two for the missing pack.

The Ironsun Pack. The one Velina made clear that she hated.

We received limited applause, and when we arrived at our seats, I thought the doors would close and the opening ceremony would start. I'd assumed the other pack just wasn't coming.

I was wrong.

Alpha Ivan tensed next to me, a sound of disgust leaving him as a final announcement was made: "And finally, we would like to welcome the Ironsun Pack, represented by Ravik Gentry."

Ravik. My gaze slowly rose from my lap to see who belonged to the name that had caught my attention. Not just mine, but my wolf's as well.

A sound like cracking thunder echoed in my ears as something fractured inside me, breaking loose. Something that wanted to rush forward, to *greet* this man...

this *Ravik*. I felt breathless, frozen as golden eyes locked with mine from across the room.

An explosion of heat bloomed through my chest, my heart pounding so violently it made me tremble. The world turned fuzzy around the edges, and molten energy invaded my limbs, making my fingers tingle.

The power Ravik carried was unlike anything I'd ever felt. And as he strode through the double doors, his massive stature seeming to shrink the space, his gaze never left mine.

Easily in his late twenties, the man carried himself like a king. The room roared in applause at his presence, but he barely seemed to notice. Instead he was completely focused on me, and I allowed myself a breathless second to appreciate how beautiful he was.

Ravik's golden skin seemed to warm under the light that streamed through the windows. His jaw was covered in a neat beard the same color as the chocolate-toned waves of his hair, which shimmered faintly with gold. He wore a blood red military uniform accented with gold, and his crest—a dangerous-looking wolf—stood proudly on the right side of his chest.

I'd never seen, or experienced, anyone like him before.

Who was this man?

CHAPTER 6
RAVIK

THOSE EYES... They were gold, yes, but deeper. Burnished with sorrow, fractured with defiance just beneath the surface. Our gazes clashed. I refused to look away. The rest of the room disappeared as a glow seemed to rise from her skin, her aura pulsing with power. Divine. Eternal. Who was this woman?

A shock of red hair—striking, even pinned back— had me crossing the room without hesitation, needing to lock onto her scent so I could never forget it. Never forget her.

I ignored the greetings of the other territory leaders, rounding the table with one goal in mind—taking my place beside her. She tracked my approach, but the moment my chair scraped back, she flinched.

I froze. Confusion twisted in my chest.

Her eyes—so vibrant just moments ago—were

now lowered. She ducked her head, hiding behind silence. How was that possible? She had to feel it—the same pull, the same recognition.

Mine.

"Ravik Gentry." My name on his tongue was a violation. I snapped my gaze up, a growl curling in my chest as I registered the man beside her—Alpha Ivan. I narrowed my gaze on his amused expression and the way his hand was placed on the back of *her* chair. As if she belonged to him. My wolf howled in response to that.

Impossible.

"Ivan."

I wouldn't call him Alpha—*ever*. My father hadn't, and I planned on following suit.

The woman's scent wrapped around me like a blanket of silk, vanilla twisted with cinnamon. My fists clenched. I couldn't reach out and touch her—I couldn't risk her flinching again.

"She draws attention, I'll admit." Ivan's words were twisted with cruelty. "But trust me, she's not worth your curiosity."

The words made her physically shrink, recoiling as if she'd been hit. My eyes narrowed on the bastard. "I will decide what and who is worth my curiosity."

Sitting down, I ignored Ivan and instead focused on the small woman next to me. She couldn't have been more than 5'2", and her silhouette, cloaked in thick material, seemed slight. Too small. She was absolutely beautiful, but certain details stood out to me—crimson flags of warning.

Bruises along the back of her neck, as if someone had been gripping there. Her fingers were tinged with purple—faint blotches not yet healed. Her body trembled as if she were trying to contain something, locking everything down in an attempt at practiced perfection. Somehow I knew that if she looked at me, if I could see her face, I would see *everything*.

My wolf slammed against his cage, savage and bloodthirsty, demanding retribution. My hands curled into fists, ready to massacre whoever had dared break her like this.

"What's your name, *lux mea*?"

My light.

"*Lux mea*?" she echoed, her eyes darting up before her lips pressed tight, as if she hadn't meant to speak at all. Luckily, Ivan was being entertained by some woman positioned between him and that sick twisted freak Graeme.

"*My light*." I answered easily—because that is exactly what she was. A vibrant flame that Ivan was attempting to extinguish. I didn't care who he thought she was to him. He was wrong.

A pink blush filled her cheeks, her shoulders relaxing as she turned toward me.

"You shouldn't be calling me that," she said quietly, her hands tightening and twisting in her lap.

"Then tell me your name," I demanded softly.

"Gracie," she whispered.

A name soft and sweet, but somehow perfectly hers.

"Gracie, look at me." My voice was hoarse from the tension I was holding in my own frame. She slowly drew her eyes up once more, a sparkle of magic playing in the golden iris. The room buzzed with idle conversation, but none of it mattered. Not when her voice was the only sound I cared about. "Do you belong to Ivan?"

Her eyes rounded and her lips parted. A breath, sharp and unsure, slipped out like a confession trapped beneath fear. "No. He has two mates. I...don't belong anywhere."

But she did. She absolutely fucking did—she belonged here, with me. Gracie had answered my question, but she'd revealed far more. A strong wave of protectiveness, of possessiveness, punched me in the gut as I fought the need to pull her onto my lap, to shelter her from the oppressive weight that was so obviously closing in on her.

"Why are you here?" I asked seriously. The question made her wince. I didn't know the reason, but I would unearth it. I would figure out why she was so damn afraid.

"Ravik, it's wonderful to see you." A familiar voice on my other side drew my attention. Alpha Lacey Harrison sat on her own—her assistant, who was always next to her, notably gone.

I gave her a nod of greeting before looking back to Gracie, only to find her attention on Lacey as well. I tilted my head with curiosity, seeing something there. Annoyance? Frustration? She didn't say anything, but her expression said a lot.

"It's a shame your father couldn't make it. Alpha Deegan is always a joy to be around," she continued, and I realized I was going to have to say something to the insufferable woman. I wasn't the only one who felt that way, either—almost everyone in the eight territories disliked her. Not as much as they disliked Ivan, but still a fair amount.

"There's a lot to handle back home," I offered. "The transition of power is a responsibility he takes seriously."

"Yes, I heard that," she mused, taking a sip of wine. I knew that our host would be making a speech any minute here, and I really wanted to talk to Gracie more. Unfortunately, Lacey didn't give a shit.

"I also heard he was sick. Is that true?"

I contained the defensive growl stuck in my throat and provided a forced yet polite smile. "No."

Except that was a lie—one I didn't mind telling. I

was curious how she even knew that piece of information, considering how tight-lipped we were keeping it.

"Oh, good." She sighed. "Where are the other two who are always by your side? I do enjoy that one... Basir, is it?"

"Busy." My answers were growing sharper as I felt annoyance curl off of Gracie. I didn't understand her reaction completely, and I wasn't deluded enough to think she didn't like me talking to Lacey for the same reasons I wouldn't want her talking to another man.

Enough of Lacey Harrison. I turned back to Gracie and found her already watching me from beneath her lashes, her expression more open now that Ivan was across the room speaking to our host.

"I really shouldn't be talking to you, especially when he's around," she expressed, her voice warm and delicate.

By The Eight, this woman was almost too much to be around. Everything about her was appealing, to the point that she was intoxicating. It was like Vorrakar had hand-crafted the perfect woman for me, forging her in his fires and placing her in front of me.

She continued, "I'm not trying to be rude, but I was told not to talk."

"He told you not to talk?"

"To you and some others. I...I shouldn't have even told you that."

"Hey." I captured her chin. At my touch, a shiver

rolled over her, her eyes dilating as her wolf reached out to me. I nearly fucking forgot what I was going to say. "You can tell me anything, Gracie."

The sound of a chair being yanked back had Gracie jumping away from me, nearly hurting herself in the process. Graeme chuckled from a few seats away as she shrank into herself. He'd done it on purpose. A vicious noise escaped from my throat, and my hand darted out to rest on Gracie's lower back.

Graeme's voice was harsh. "Don't play with things that don't belong to you, Ravik. Remember, your old man sent you here for business, not pleasure."

Something about his words had Gracie's brows knitting together as she leaned forward to escape my touch. I loathed that. Some form of reality had destroyed the innate closeness and familiarity she'd felt toward me, and now I felt as though we were leagues apart. I wouldn't have another moment to correct it, either, as Ivan returned to his seat and the opening ceremonies began.

"Honored Alphas and esteemed delegates, on behalf of the Scarlet Sloth Territory, I welcome you to the Fifty-Third Thornfell Trade Conference."

I looked for Basir and Thornar in the room, but I couldn't find either.

I had no doubt they were doing their part in all this. After all, we were the only three representatives for the Ironsun Pack here—but with Gracie next to me, I needed another set of eyes on everything.

Alpha Kaliyah continued, "We are incredibly grateful for your presence and humbled to be selected to host this year's gathering—especially in a season of reflection and harvest from a long year of work. This year, we meet to not only discuss trade and treaty, but to reaffirm the alliances that unite Thornfell."

If this was Thornfell united, I feared what divided would look like. I noticed Gracie seemed captivated by her words, and despite not knowing anything about her situation outside of rumors on how Alpha Ivan ran his pack, I got the distinct impression that she hadn't been to an event like this. Ever. It made me view the moment through a different lens.

"So let us speak not as rivals but as servants of our people, bound by the duty to make our territories and nation greater. Let us begin this conference with open minds and a shared desire for the growth of Thornfell."

Polite applause and cheers sounded as people raised their glasses in toast, and the kitchen doors opened to serve food and drinks to those gathered.

Gracie's head was moving around the room on a swivel, as if trying to take everything in, while nervously tapping her fingers against her lap. I wanted to place my much larger hand over them, to still the internal race in her head that I could see playing out.

I should have been focused on talking about steel contracts and expanding our mines, but all I could focus on was the way her eyes went wide in surprise at the food placed in front of her. She didn't even move to touch her silverware at first.

"Eat." Ivan's words were a sharp directive, and I didn't stop the rumble that escaped my chest this time. A massive smile grew on his face. He'd been waiting for that.

"If I'd known you had interest, Ravik, I would have considered you a potential option for her future," he mused. Anger grew in my chest at his implication. "Then again, I would have assumed your father would be here. I suppose the old man probably couldn't handle the travel though."

Ivan's jab didn't faze me. He was less than a quarter of the man my father was, even in his current state.

"You know..." Ivan put down his silverware and leaned over Gracie, making her drop her bite of food before it even reached her mouth. "I could still arrange for something, maybe. Even if it's just one night with my little pet here."

Malice leaked from my response. "I suppose that answers my question on whether she's here by choice. I've heard your pack is filled with women who aren't offered any choices."

Ivan chuckled, his eyes flashing with venom.

"Maybe. Maybe not. That doesn't really fucking matter since they belong to me."

That was the issue—it did matter. Gracie mattered, and it was pretty damn clear why.

As Ivan went back to talking to Graeme, I kept my gaze on Gracie as she picked up her fork and took a hesitant bite of food, her body sinking against the chair to make herself as small as possible. I knew there was so much more to her, like a flame that was on the verge of being extinguished.

I wanted to watch her glow.

"Gracie—"

She flinched at the sound of her name, lifting her gaze with eyes rimmed in exhaustion.

"Please don't," she whispered. "Please leave it alone...leave me alone."

Gracie didn't realize that wasn't a possibility.

I couldn't walk away from *lux mea*.

CHAPTER 7
GRACIE

"THESE SCARS ARE HIDEOUS." Velina's analysis didn't cut as deep as I would have expected. Her critical eye scanned over my dress—or more like what my dress revealed. Even her hurtful words couldn't completely ruin my mood, though.

For the past six hours and twenty-seven minutes, I'd been in paradise.

Or the closest to paradise that someone like me could hope to find.

Following the lunch that Alpha Ivan had all but dragged me from, ranting about my interactions with Ravik, I had assumed the worst—that I would be punished for my actions. Considering the fury on Ravik's face, I think he assumed that would be the case as well. I'd watched helplessly as he tried to move past the wall of soldiers Ivan had erected before he whisked me out of sight.

I'd been filled with fear and dread, yet still dizzy from the high of simply sharing the same air as Ravik. I was intoxicated by the man and his scent of fresh linen and steel. Cold. Hard. Unyielding. Yet somehow familiar to me. It made me want to bury my head against his chest, just for a moment.

It was a ridiculous thought, and I'm sure if he could see into my thoughts, he would think the same. The man barely knew me, yet I was fantasizing about being held by him.

What was wrong with me?

It was a question I'd actually had a lot of time to ponder while Alpha Ivan attended meeting after meeting without me. Since he didn't approve of my actions during my first public outing, he'd promptly dumped me in the room, locking the door and leaving me surrounded by the luxury of the hotel suite.

The relief I felt at being temporarily safe was unmatched.

Velina hadn't said a word, just shot me a look that said she pitied me almost as much as she despised me. She hated what I reminded her of—that we were both property.

Instead of trying to talk to her, I hid in one of the many rooms to...rest. I'd even napped. I soaked in the oversized tub, flipping through channels just to see what the world was watching now. I couldn't remember a time when I'd been able to relax for so long.

When Velina ordered three women to "prepare" me for the evening, I'd barely managed to hide my disappointment. I'd hoped somehow that Ivan would keep me locked away in here, able to just *be*. The only positive was that I'd learned there would be two more sessions of meetings, which meant there was a potential for more rest in my future.

"I didn't pick the dress," I pointed out, reminding her that I'd been forced into the gown that showcased the marks on my side. She was right, anyway—the puckered skin clashed brutally with the luxurious garment.

The ivory piece had flowing silk sleeves and a high neckline that covered my body in a smooth sheath down to where it pooled gently at my feet. I felt as though I was wrapped in a cloud of luxury, and it would have been wonderful...if not for the completely open back.

Alpha Ivan was probably trying to ensure I looked alluring, that I served my purpose...but he didn't know about the scars. They were at least half visible.

Shame colored my cheeks. They must look really horrible to evoke such a reaction from Velina, so strong that it had escaped her control to write itself so clearly upon her face. If she felt that way, it meant others would. It meant that *Ravik* would. I'd never felt embarrassed by my scars before, but I'd also kept them hidden, never asked to flaunt them.

I internally chastised myself. My scars meant I was a survivor, and what did I care about the opinion of a man who...well, what did he do? Unfortunately, far too much to me.

I'd been mesmerized by his presence. Intimidated, yet absolutely in awe. I could feel him all around me, and when he touched me in the simplest way, I melted, my body turning into magma. It had only been the very real threat made by Alpha Ivan that had broken the trance—that made me realize I was putting Ravik in danger simply by interacting with him.

I would shield him from Alpha Ivan's fury.

Those had been the easier emotions to identify—the strong sense of protectiveness and, of course, lust. My body had felt electrified at his mere attention, to the point that I had felt electrified and breathless.

The emotion that had shocked and confused me the most, though?

Possessiveness. When Lacey Harrison had talked to him, I'd felt... angry. Her tone of voice had annoyed me, along with the way she'd kept grasping at his attention, trying to draw him away from me.

I didn't have a right to hold his attention. I normally avoided attention, so it would only make sense that the man whose attention I *did* want was so...everything I wasn't. Ravik shone with life and power, radiating strength. I was a shell compared to him, and I felt selfish for wanting to bask within his aura.

So I wouldn't allow myself to consider what he would think about how I looked tonight. I shouldn't be thinking about him at all. It was horrible of me to put him in Ivan's crosshairs because I couldn't control myself.

"Gracie." Velina's voice snapped me into the present. "You're not listening, girl."

"I was thinking about what you said."

"Right. Well, that is the dress Alpha Ivan wants you to wear, so it will have to do. Hopefully you'll be good enough for what we're trying to achieve."

It was painful, having another woman treat me like an object, only valuable if I could gain the approval of Alpha Waylon. It was clear that everything rested on my ability to...charm him? Seduce him? I couldn't fathom how to do either of those.

The walk down to the ballroom was quiet. Velina's steps were quick and impatient as I tried to follow the best I could, glad they had only put me in small heels. The way the dress pooled on the ground didn't help my ability to walk confidently, and I was uncomfortable by the time we reached the hallway outside the ballroom, feeling more than a bit shaky. Alpha Ivan waited off to the side of the entrance, looking annoyed.

"Alpha Ivan, sorry about the delay. We had to address an issue."

Alpha Ivan had changed into formal wear, displaying the Cold Moon Pack crest in embroidered stitching along the back of his navy-blue jacket—something I could only see because of the gilded mirror he stood in front of, reflecting the candlelight throughout the hall. He was tapping his fingers against his side as if he was nervous...about tonight? About his plans? I had no idea.

"What issue?" he demanded.

"Scars," Velina said, nodding toward my side. Ivan's face transformed into disgust as he eyed me like I was trash underneath his feet.

"You have a deformity? No one informed me of this."

A deformity? I suppose it was...although I'd hardly go to that extent.

"We could change her dress for tonight and hope he doesn't notice," Velina suggested as Ivan walked around me, looking over me with a critical evaluation that had anxiety welling up inside of me

Alpha Ivan shook his head. "No—she will have to do as is. Come. Now."

I followed him silently, feeling as though I was leashed. Like some kind of animal. As we stepped into the ballroom, I realized dinner had already begun, and my eyes darted throughout the room in search of one person: Ravik.

Alpha Ivan's hand wrapped around my arm like a vise, pulling me close to speak in a dark tone near my ear. "There is only one voice you'll answer to tonight—mine. Let your attention stray from our goal, and I'll make sure you remember where your loyalties lie."

Nodding once, I kept my gaze down until he pulled back a chair, ordering me to sit. Immediately, I knew that Ravik was nowhere near me. This setup was different than at lunch. We sat at tables with our own 'delegates,' which meant Clint and Marek were closest to us. Unfortunately, the latter was on my left.

"I heard you were talking to the Gentry boy earlier." Marek chuckled. "You know what they say—dirt attracts dirt." It suddenly became hard to breathe through the need to defend Ravik, to let out a growl at Marek, to demand he take it back.

"Heard his father is sick," he continued. "Will probably need to take over soon, once the old man kicks the bucket. Deegan deserves it, as far as I'm concerned—always preaching about right and wrong as if he's better than us."

I had no idea what Alpha Deegan was like, but I could sense Ravik was good. Or at least I wanted to believe that. Maybe everyone seemed good compared to the Cold Moon Pack.

Marek, giving up on trying to talk to me, resorted

to gripping my thigh in a hard hold before turning to talk to someone on his other side. I tried to pull my leg free, but his grip turned bruising. I stilled, not willing to risk drawing his or Ivan's anger right now. Even my wolf locked up, paralyzed by the memory of pain, unsure whether to growl or cower. We'd learned that fighting back never worked in this pack.

Eventually, his hand released my leg as he stood to greet someone approaching from our left. I let out a small breath of relief in the moment before Alpha Ivan spoke directly to me.

"Alpha Waylon. You will talk to him tonight. You will do everything in your power to hold his attention. Understand?"

My gaze moved to the Alpha he was talking about, and I noted his observant gaze as he nodded in conversation with one of his soldiers.

"Okay."

It was all I could offer as we were served our first course of dinner, my attention turning to the rest of the room. To the strong display of flags and crests, the luxurious material that coated each guest, and the way the crystal chandeliers reflected the candlelight. To the warm scent of delicious food and the band playing soft music. It felt like...well, not exactly a dream, but not my real life. I had never, even before the raid, experienced beauty like this. I may have been caged, trapped in Alpha Ivan's prison, but that meant

I appreciated what lay outside of those bars even more.

Two courses later, between Marek continuously trying to touch me as he spoke to others and the weight of Alpha Ivan's presence, I began to feel light-headed. It didn't help that I'd yet to see Ravik. I wasn't even sure he was here.

No. That wasn't true. I may not have been able to see him, but I could feel him.

Realizing I was going to pass out if I didn't get some fresh air, I slowly pushed my chair back. Instantly, Alpha Ivan caught my wrist. I spoke softly, trying to excuse myself. "I need to use the bathroom."

His lip curled as he addressed Clint. "Go. Make sure she doesn't get herself into trouble." At least it wasn't Marek.

Luckily, the room was crowded enough that Clint couldn't talk to me, let alone stand next to me, as I made my way toward the attendant at the front of the hall. They directed me toward the bathroom, and I let out a breath of relief once I was safely inside. The room was huge, with four smaller rooms attached that I knew were actual bathrooms, while this main space had couches and served as a powder room.

I selected the door on the furthest side of the room, locking myself inside. Still facing the door, I wilted under the relief of being alone. My forehead pressed against the cold surface as I closed my eyes, inhaling the sterile scent of the bathroom mixed with lavender candles.

The peaceful moment lulled my anxiety just enough that I began to feel more stable, less light-headed. I knew *why* I felt this way: the expectations weighing on me were too much. If I didn't get this right—if I messed this up in Alpha Ivan's eyes—there would be hell to pay.

Maybe I could escape. Just climb out a window and run away. I could feel a cool breeze coming from somewhere, but it wasn't until the scent of smoke tickled my nose that I turned to look around...

And stopped dead in my tracks.

A man sat on the windowsill, watching me.

A storm surged through my veins, and I felt as if I'd been punched in the chest. My knees felt weak, and the breath whooshed out of me as the man's magic coasted against my skin in greeting. His power tasted different from Ravik's but was equally as strong as his scent wrapped around me: gunpowder and sandalwood.

"What..." I stumbled over my words, moving back as my heart rapidly beat in my ears, unable to slow. "How...how did you get there?"

The man was large—nearly Ravik's height—and made of lean, cut muscles that I could see underneath the black shirt that molded to his chest and arms. In fact, he was covered in black, and though the clothes were simple, I could tell they were expensive. Everything about the man screamed wealth and luxury, down to the gold-lined grayscale tattoos that wrapped down his arms and peeked over the collar of his shirt. I caught imagery of the sun but quickly moved my eyes up to his face, which was completely blank—devoid of expression.

"Through the door, much like yourself." His voice was rough and gravelly, and I swallowed nervously. His emerald gaze didn't miss the motion, and his eyes darkened. He clearly didn't like how I was acting; I just didn't understand why. Or, more importantly, why he was *here*.

"Why are you in here?"

For a moment, the man said nothing, languidly moving his left arm out the window and dropping his cigarette. I hadn't even realized he'd been smoking, too absorbed in his presence alone. As he moved his gaze back to me, I couldn't help but notice that he seemed to be trying to tone down his energy, softening it.

Was that for me? I tightened my hands at my sides, wondering why he was trying to appear less terrifying when he was so extremely intimidating. Even if his black, shoulder-length hair looked extremely soft— my fingers itching to run through it.

I had to stop. Just because I was attracted to

someone didn't mean I should have such an extreme reaction. This was insanity.

"Do you often sit in the girls' bathroom?" I demanded, picking my chin up and forcing myself to ask the questions I needed answers to. I wouldn't flee. Every moment I was near Alpha Ivan was spent cowering. I wouldn't do that right now. My wolf let out a silent rumble of agreement, moving through my chest with a determined stride, trying to show just how dangerous we could be.

Considering the man's wolf was nowhere to be found, I knew we weren't intimidating him in the least.

"No, I don't, Gracie."

"How do you know my name?"

"It's my job to keep an eye on everyone and everything." He stood slowly, straightening his spine, and in a second flat he was in my space, backing me up against the door.

The air seemed to buzz around me, and my eyes grew heavy as he put his arms on either side of me, never touching me. Simply looking me over.

"I don't understand—"

The man dipped his head, brushing his lips across my cheek. The action, the barest touch, had my knees nearly breaking as I reached out to grip onto him. A pained noise came from his throat as he steadied me and stepped back. As far away as he could from me, back by the window.

What...what had just happened? My heart hurt at his distance, my hands gripping the door as I tried to slow my breathing. I watched as he eased himself through the bathroom window onto a ledge above a moat-like channel I had noticed circling the building upon arrival. Even on the main floor, the drop was enough to make my stomach twist. Panic slammed into my chest as he swung himself down, disappearing from view.

When I ran over to the window and looked down, I saw no sign of him.

Who was that?

Clint's voice suddenly echoed in the room. "Gracie. Out, now."

Nodding, I hurried from the room and allowed him to walk me back into the ballroom, still in a daze. It hadn't felt as though I'd been in there for long at all, but when I saw that dinner was over and everyone was moving around, I understood Clint's annoyance with me.

Alpha Ivan stood as we approached, his eyes narrowing on me.

"Sorry."

"Quiet. Let's go."

I walked next to him as he led me onto the floor, no

doubt to meet Waylon. But as we approached, my steps hesitated until I came to a stop.

My hearing went out, dancing with the noise of my own heartbeat, as my vision narrowed in on the two of them at the far side of the room...watching me. Ravik and the other man. Both from the Ironsun Pack. Why hadn't he said anything?

Alpha Ivan's hand locked around the back of my neck, ripping my attention away from the two men as I was pushed toward Alpha Waylon. How was I supposed to talk to a man that didn't hold my interest when there were two who did only feet away? My wolf howled in my ears at my forced redirection.

Alpha Ivan's grip reminded me *how*: my life was on the line.

CHAPTER 8
GRACIE

It was clear to me why Alpha Ivan wanted to earn Alpha Waylon's respect and become trading partners. While I didn't understand what made an alpha good, it was obvious that the people of the Stark Flight, who stood all around him, not only authentically liked him, but he seemed vested in what they were telling him. He had a relaxed, friendly disposition that still retained the certainty required for his position.

So when we finally reached him, I was surprised by the sudden turn in his demeanor. His face remained friendly, but I saw the disdain in his gaze.

"Alpha Waylon, just the man I was looking for." Alpha Ivan's voice was filled with a smarmy self-assuredness that made me feel sick to my stomach. I hoped for Alpha Waylon's sake that he could read between the lines and see how fake it was. Considering the way he looked at Alpha Ivan, I had a feeling he did.

Which, of course, didn't bode well for my situation.

"Yes, I heard you were coming," Alpha Waylon said, his gaze moving over to me briefly with a nod of greeting. "And this must be your mate."

"No," Alpha Ivan instantly corrected. "Gracie is one of our most promising pack members and has a vested interest in trade politics, so I wanted to give her the opportunity to experience the TTC in all of its glory." The last part was said with a bit of amusement, and I couldn't help but make a face, looking down to hide it. An interest in trade politics? I had an interest in staying alive past tomorrow, but politics...

"Interesting. I didn't see her in the meetings," Alpha Waylon commented. "Nonetheless, it's good to meet you, Gracie."

My gaze moved up to his as I offered a small nod. "Great to meet you as well."

"Right. Well, if you don't mind, Ivan—"

"I wanted to talk to you about something before we continue to enjoy the night," Alpha Ivan interrupted.

"I would rather save deal-making for the morning," Alpha Waylon said, again trying to dismiss us. My cheeks turned hot in embarrassment. Ivan had no shame, but *I* did.

Alpha Ivan's energy turned darker, more malice-filled, as he spoke with a quiet but harder edge. "This isn't the type of deal you make at the table, Waylon."

Instantly, the dragon's entire disposition changed. He straightened up further, his gaze narrowing on Alpha Ivan before moving to me. I tried to stay perfectly still, not wanting to disrupt the moment or ruin his analysis of me.

"Is it?" Alpha Waylon looked back at Alpha Ivan. "And what exactly do you want, Ivan?"

"Trade routes open between our territories. Surely an alpha of your experience can see the value of what's in front of you."

Bile rose in my throat as I looked down at the floor, trying to calm my heartbeat. The chuckle that left Alpha Waylon was filled with a sharp disgust that had my eyes widening in surprise. Alpha Waylon spoke louder than before. "Trying to trade a girl to me—especially one who's younger than my own grand-niece—is a foul move, even for you, Ivan. The Stark Flight has not traded with the Cold Moon Pack since its inception, and I continue to maintain that we will not work with a regime that traffics broken shifters."

Alpha Ivan's wolf exploded in fury, a savage sound breaking from his throat. The force behind it made me tremble involuntarily, but all I felt was relief. Humiliation at being rejected as well, but mostly an easing in my chest. I kept my expression neutral as I waited on

Alpha Ivan, not wanting to show any sign of the reprieve I'd been given.

Alpha Ivan chuckled, his disposition remaining the picture of relaxed despite his wolf's behavior. "You take yourself far too seriously, old man. I simply wanted to talk—but it's clear you don't have the stomach to grow in power."

Alpha Ivan's hand wrapped around my arm, and I was pulled violently from the Stark Flight table and toward the door. A whimper left me as his grip turned merciless. His violent fury filled the air, turning it so hot I could barely breathe. The relief I'd felt was suddenly replaced by terror.

He would kill me.

We didn't even make it back to our suite. He used his bulk to crowd me into a room near the stairwell, the door slamming shut behind us. I backed as far away as I could, listening as his soldiers positioned themselves in front of the door to keep anyone from interrupting us. The backs of my calves hit into a couch, and I gasped as I fumbled in the dark to keep myself upright.

Alpha Ivan was silent, pacing back and forth near the door as I tried to gauge what was going to happen. Nothing good. Nothing good at all.

"You had one job," he hissed, approaching me. "One fucking job, and you couldn't even do that right."

"I didn't even have a chance to say—"

Alpha Ivan's hand wrapped around my throat, cutting off my air supply. I knew I shouldn't have spoken, but it had been my last-ditch attempt to make him see the truth—to make him see that this wasn't my fault. His grasp turned tighter as he moved in my face, overpowering and overshadowing me.

"What a waste of time. A pathetic excuse for a wolf," he snarled, lifting me from the floor. I flailed, trying to remove his hand from my throat. When he tossed me to the side, I slammed into a chair, my head throbbing in pain as I slid to the floor. Using the side of his boot, he rolled me onto my back and stepped right on my chest, eyeing me like I was prey already bleeding out.

"I should have known that a piece of shit like you wouldn't hold the attention of an alpha," he spit, his foot compressing on my chest. When he lifted it, I tried to roll over, gasping for air, but he kicked me hard in the ribs, finally tearing a cry from my throat. I pressed my lips together as he grabbed the back of my neck and pulled me up, moving his hands into my hair and ripping at it violently.

"So what do I do with you now?" he growled, dropping me down on the couch. I tried to back away from him but he grabbed my jaw, squeezing so hard it felt as though it would break. Tears leaked down my face as a smile grew on his lips, getting sick pleasure out of my fear. "Answer."

"I can go back to the kitchen—"

"No," he snarled, using his free hand to slap me hard across the face, my head aching from the force behind the hit. "You'll be useful in some way or another. Maybe I'll give you to Marek."

A whimper of fear escaped my throat.

His hold on me released as he stood, yet again looking down on me. "No, I wouldn't give my third-in-command such vile trash. Go, Gracie. Back to the room. Tell Velina to prepare for us to leave tomorrow. You've made this trip utterly pointless."

I didn't hesitate, sprinting for the door as he ordered his soldiers to open it. I tripped over my dress as I stepped out, falling to the ground and slamming my nose into the stone. I whimpered as the scent of blood filled the air, and Marek laughed. At that point I realized I hadn't tripped...he had put his foot out.

Gathering my dress and kicking off my shoes, I stood and ran. I didn't look back because that would only slow me down, and Alpha Ivan's men would be looking for excuses to punish me. I would seek refuge back in the hotel room. After running down two long hallways without hearing anyone coming after me, I slowed.

Exhaustion and adrenaline roared inside of me, equally pulling at me as my body slumped against the wall. I pushed myself to keep moving, though. I was bloody and bruised, and I felt like prey. I *was* prey to them. It had never been more clear than now.

My wolf was silent, curled up inside of me, unwilling to make a stand or even a move against such anger. We had limits, and this was it. I couldn't be strong even if I wanted to. Fear tormented every part of me, and when I reached a door, I pressed against it, knowing that it would lead to the emergency stairwell.

The cold hallway was a relief against my skin and would keep me hidden. Our room was on the sixth floor, five floors up, but for now I just...sat down. A floor-to-ceiling window to my left revealed a refracted image of me in the shadows of the nighttime city.

Blood stained my ivory gown, the bottom ripped from my fall. My face was colored with blood from my nose, and faint purple bruises were beginning to form on my jaw and throat. I cleared my throat, not even sure if I could talk. What would Velina think?

It didn't matter—not really. Somehow, I knew she'd been through worse.

Suddenly, a shadow moved across the stairs as someone came jogging down, their footsteps heavy. Curling into the wall, I tried to remain invisible...until a blanket of warmth wrapped around me. My body froze in recognition as the power soothed my injured flesh and the scent of brown sugar and bourbon tickled my senses.

I didn't have the energy to look up as they

approached me from behind, their body casting such a large shadow that it should have terrified me. Instead, all I felt was need. I *needed* to see who this was, even if I looked horrific, I *needed* to connect the power to the man walking toward me. Adrenaline coursed through my veins, turning my fingertips cold, and my heart began to beat loud and demanding in my ears as I tried to look up.

Chocolate brown eyes circled with gold. At some point the massive man had crouched behind me, so he was at eye level as he looked over me in surprise, shock, and...something else. Something darker. His coiled onyx hair was cut in a fade, longer on top than on the sides, and his smooth skin had undertones of gold and fire beneath the bronze. *He was beautiful— unfairly beautiful.*

A brilliant smile graced his face. I must have accidentally said that last thought aloud. "Listen, little flame, if you're going to say stuff like that, I'm going to assume we're getting married. Doesn't seem very fair since I don't know your name."

Oh. Oh wow. Even his voice was perfect, like honey. I think I may have been losing too much blood at this point because...

The world around me went dark.

WHEN I WOKE, I was held in a pair of muscular arms, my head resting against the man's chest. I breathed in his scent as he spoke from above me, his tone rougher than before.

"Hang in there. We're going to make sure you get looked at."

That couldn't happen. If Alpha Ivan found out...

The world blinked out of focus again, and when I woke this time, the bright lights of the stairwell were gone. I was still resting against the man's chest, and I could hear one other person nearby. They spoke quietly in low, distinct tones, and I could sense a familiar power right within reach.

"They're coming for her." The man from the bath-room. I opened my eyes again and found myself looking directly up at him. I couldn't tell where we were—it wasn't a hotel room like I'd assumed, but more like a lounge area. Couches and tables were just within my peripheral vision.

"You again," I whispered.

"Why am I not surprised that you've met Basir," the man holding me drawled in amusement. "How are you feeling, little flame?"

"Is that your name? Basir?" I asked the man across from me. As if me saying his name was painful, his jaw tightened before he offered a nod. Not a word left his lips, but as his gaze moved over my lips and down to my throat, I saw something burn behind his eyes—a simple spark that could easily turn into an inferno.

Basir. I liked that name. A lot. Looking up at the second man, I found a charming smirk on his lips as he gazed back at me. Despite how horrifying I probably looked, covered in blood and bruises, he didn't look at me like that...he looked at me differently than I'd experienced before. Something about the way he held me tugged at the back of my mind. A warning? Or encouragement to get closer to him? I really didn't know.

"Thornar," he introduced himself. "And you must be Gracie. Ravik mentioned you."

"You both know him?" I croaked, looking back and forth between them.

"Know him? I work for him." Thornar winked. "But yeah, the bastard is like a brother."

This man was so full of life, he was like sunshine on a rainy day. I wanted to revel in it. And Basir, he was the coolest night, wrapping around you at the end of a long day.

"Less than a minute," Basir warned. "We have to let her go. He's the one coming for her."

I looked at Basir, feeling a surge of knowing panic as Thornar let out a low rumble of disapproval. My voice was raspy as I tried to get out my question. "Who—"

"Gracie." Alpha Ivan's sharp tone had my entire body trembling. I scrambled out of Thornar's arms, making him curse as I tried to distance myself as much as possible. I nearly fell over in the effort, my ribs echoing with pain as my pulse beat wildly in my throat, my gaze darting around to watch Ivan and his soldiers approaching.

I didn't want the two of them to be punished because of the state I was in. I didn't want Alpha Ivan's wrath turned on them.

"Alpha Ivan." Thornar's voice was filled with disgust as he gently helped me stand.

Alpha Ivan ignored him. "Come, Gracie. We're done with tonight."

"She needs medical attention. We were waiting on our—"

"No." Alpha Ivan laughed as he approached and grabbed my arm. "Come now, Gracie."

Before we could move an inch, Basir blocked our path out of the room, pointedly eyeing Alpha Ivan's grip on me as he spoke in a quiet but steady tone. "She needs help."

"I will decide what she needs," Alpha Ivan snarled. "And I won't have a Gentry lackey tell me what to do with my property. She deserved every one of those injuries."

I could see it register with Basir that Alpha Ivan had been the one to do *this* to me. His eyes went cold as true darkness enveloped him.

In a fast move, I was whisked away from the

confrontation and placed within the wall of bodies that Ivan had brought with him. *Ivan hadn't come alone.* In fact, he seemed to need thirty men to do this particular job.

"Don't start something you can't finish, boys. She's not worth it."

I kept my gaze forward, tears crowding my eyes. I heard Thornar say my name from behind the wave of men, but I couldn't bring myself to look back—to watch the expression of two of the men that had made me feel so much in so little time. I was afraid they'd see the truth in Alpha Ivan's words.

That I wasn't worth anything.

But somewhere deep inside, my wolf stirred.

Why didn't we fully believe him anymore?

CHAPTER 9
BASIR

IN MY TWENTY-FIVE years of life, I'd experienced horrific things. Moments that would turn the stomach of a seasoned soldier. Moments that would reduce your hope in humanity to ashes. Somehow, because of the glowing woman being stolen from me, this moment would be the one imprinted on my tarnished soul.

Gracie didn't even fight.

The wall of men in front of me were itching for battle, but if I raised my knife now, it would be a slaughter. In the five minutes that we'd been alone with her, I'd memorized every bruise along her jaw and throat. I'd studied the way the blood from her nose stained her porcelain skin and silk dress. I'd watched her labored, heavy breathing as her trembling hand subconsciously grasped at her bruised ribs.

Our medical team hadn't gotten there in time.

Alpha Ivan had had his ears to the ground, watching Gracie close enough that we'd barely had any time with her. And now she was gone.

My fingers tapped against the knife strapped at my hip as I found myself calculating how fast I would have to move to make sure all of them were bleeding out before they could call for reinforcements.

Thornar's hand on my shoulder brought me back to the present. He nodded to the right—to the door of our suite.

I understood what he was saying; I just wasn't sure I could walk away.

Even if it was for a mere minute to disperse these other soldiers.

Inhaling sharply, I turned toward the door and forced myself inside. Thornar followed, the door echoing with a hollow thud. We should have brought her into the room. We'd been waiting on Ravik, but it had given Ivan the perfect fucking opportunity.

Thornar was calling him again, but if he wasn't picking up his phone, it was because something was going on. I watched as my brother-in-arms paced back and forth, looking far more agitated than his normal sunny disposition.

"We can't just sit here." Thornar hung up the phone, tossing it down onto the kitchenette counter. "We need to get her away from him—fuck protocol."

I could practically feel the draw down into the

depths of my own darkness as I considered what the minutes alone with Alpha Ivan would mean for Gracie. I felt like I was spiraling despite standing perfectly still, trying to keep a level of control—a level of logic. One that clearly didn't fucking apply to Gracie.

"If we take her, we risk war with Ivan and his allies. She deserves better than being the sacrificial lamb for a bloodbath he's wanted for nearly a decade." Though the words had come from my own mouth, it would take little to convince me otherwise—to act in her best interest. Thornar tried to call Ravik again, and my gaze moved past him to the windows of our suite.

Moonlight shone on the lake, one of the largest and deepest in Thornfell. Yet its depth didn't compare to the drowning sensation overwhelming me. Drowning in my darkness and the woman that inspired it. Images flashed past me as I tempered my reaction, not allowing myself to peer into that.

To truly consider what I wanted to do to her.

Removing the pocketknife from my belt, I flipped it open, smoothing my thumb over the sharpened edge. Not pressing down hard enough to draw blood, but enough to keep me in the present. I couldn't afford to snap. I couldn't afford to lose control.

Gracie had affected me from the moment Ravik mentioned her name, the draw of curiosity impossible to ignore. I'd followed her silk-covered form to the bathroom where I'd orchestrated my chance. I'd just wanted to stand in her presence, to see if her cinnamon-sugar scent was as sweet on the tongue. I hadn't wanted to feel her fear or to scare her. I hadn't even wanted to touch her.

Then I'd given into temptation and brushed my lips against her smooth, soft skin.

Gracie was...a glow. Tattoos trailed my own skin, worshipping the light—the sun—but my glow had been blessed by Vorrakar himself. Everything about her was warm, like the sensation of the summer sun on skin. Not an inferno, not an open flame. Just a warm glow, so incredibly gentle and inviting.

So incredibly dangerous.

In her state, she should have reminded me of death —of a wilting flower. Instead, she breathed life into my existence. My wolf howled in relief, as if we'd unknowingly been waiting for her.

I needed to stay far away from Gracie, to keep her safe.

Thornar threw his phone onto the couch. His reckless side was emerging, the willingness to throw himself into danger for our pack, for Ravik as his Beta —and now for Gracie. And I knew we were minutes, if not seconds, from him going rogue.

The door to our suite slammed open as Ravik entered, his gaze darting around before he swore. "Where is she? I got your text—"

"Gone," I said. "Ivan brought his men and took her.

Bastard brought thirty armed soldiers." Which meant he was both terrified of us and desperate to hang onto Gracie.

"We're going after her," Thornar bit out. "He was the one who put those marks on her skin. I don't want to imagine what he's doing now."

The three of us normally worked in flawless unison. Thornar's energetic vigor balanced my calm strategic reasoning, and Ravik led us forward. It was that simple.

But not with Gracie. Not right now.

"She's a prisoner of the Cold Moon Pack," I said, voicing what all of us knew already. "Ivan won't let her just walk away."

"I don't care," Thornar spat, getting more and more agitated.

"Continue," Ravik demanded, trying to hear me out.

"She's been in their inner circle. If she claims asylum, we could say we're extracting information from her as an informant. Everyone at this conference hates Ivan anyway, and this would allow them to justify our actions."

"We heard what Waylon said about trafficking shifters. We could say it's part of the investigation," Ravik agreed.

"I don't care what we need to tell them," Thornar

said, going to the door. "If she has another mark on her, I'm not holding back."

That was concerning...for Ivan. The three of us stormed from the room, not needing to discuss where we were going. Since meeting Gracie, we'd been well aware of where she was staying. I'd even watched her from afar for part of the afternoon. It was a wonder she hadn't caught me sitting on the balcony outside of her suite, but I hadn't wanted to disrupt her nap.

I also didn't trust myself. There was far too much I wanted to know and explore about Gracie for her to be safe alone with me. My obsession was only deepening as the seconds went by.

After we recovered her, I would keep my distance.

I *had* to keep my distance.

The room was two floors down from ours, our steps quick and silent as we moved down the service stairway. When we burst into the hotel hallway, I immediately knew something was wrong. It was far too quiet, and I didn't feel the draw that Gracie and her wolf had on me. I didn't feel that vortex-like pull—

"Gone. Fucking gone," Thornar growled from the door to their suite. The door was unlocked, the room empty, but the chaos from leaving so quickly was evident. I heard Ravik slam his fist into the wall as I made my way into the room, looking around for anything, *anything* that would explain what had happened.

"They went back. Their attempt to trade her to Waylon failed, so they left."

Ravik was right. A trace of her scent lingered, but there was nothing else. As I stepped into the bedroom, my wolf clawed at my chest. Her clothes—the ones she'd most likely come in—were scattered carelessly across the floor, like she'd been ripped away without a moment to gather anything. My jaw locked as I moved through the mess, then froze when I saw a small pouch, one that I opened quickly.

Inside, a necklace and two rings. Hers. I pressed them against my chest, a growl rising in my throat.

"We should've taken her when we had the chance. I knew she'd been injured, but I thought—fuck, I don't know what I thought," Thornar snarled. "Not that her own damn alpha hurt her."

Crouching down, I ran my fingers through droplets of blood on the tile of the bathroom. Ravik and Thornar talked in the background, plans, timing, and routes all running past me. I heard none of it. I already knew what we were going to do. My gaze followed the drops to the sink, where there was more blood and a few strands of hair.

My vision tinged red as I stood, staring at the smear of blood on the porcelain. Still fresh. My fingers ran through it—still warm.

My hand curled into a fist. My control was slipping, and I didn't care. Ivan had hurt her. *Again.*

No more. Never again.

Gracie wasn't a Cold Moon prisoner anymore. She just didn't know it yet.

CHAPTER 10
GRACIE

THE BLEAK DAWN light had me squinting in pain as I was pulled from the armored SUV and thrown onto the cold, hard ground of the compound.

When Alpha Ivan had dragged me away from Basir and Thornar, the last thing I'd expected was a pinprick of pain that made the world go black. They'd drugged me, and when I woke up in a vehicle—bound with rope around my torso, my arms pinned against me, and chains on my ankles—it was clear that the facade of civility was gone. Even Velina gave me a long glance filled with what I could almost construe as worry.

Apparently, she'd been the one to keep my unconscious form company throughout the plane ride home. I was thankful for that, especially considering how Marek had stared at me once I'd come to.

"Follow." Alpha Ivan's command echoed across

the cold, empty yard of the compound, and I managed to roll to my knees before being yanked up by the back of my neck. One of his men pushed me forward, forcing me to follow him toward one of the buildings closest to the gates—a fortress made of rusted metal.

Every step I took was painful—*past* painful. My body throbbed and my head pulsed with exhaustion, my vision turning black on the edges. My fingers were bruised, and my neck and jaw ached from the pressure Alpha Ivan had administered—almost as hard as his boot planted in the center of my chest. My blood-soaked dress stuck to me, and in the icy air sprinkled with rain, trembles wrecked my dirt-covered frame. I couldn't help but see the irony that I was still wearing the very dress that I'd been so self-conscious in before because of my scars. I had no doubt that this recent beating would leave new marks on my body, permanent ones.

I only felt moderate relief when I walked into the four walls of the building that contained our holding cells. It was where new "pack" members were brought, and I didn't even bother fighting the soldier that guided me to my new metal cage. I wanted a wall between Alpha Ivan and myself.

I stumbled to the floor as the soldier shoved me forward, and the concrete rose up to bruise my body on landing. The sound of the doors slamming shut had me turning on my knees to face Ivan, who stood in a shadow outside of my prison, staring at me with pure contempt.

Ice coated his venomous tone as he spoke in a clipped, hard voice. "You failed. You embarrassed me. We went for one singular purpose, and you served *no* purpose."

My wolf let out a low rumble in my chest, but I didn't rise to my own defense. Alpha Ivan may have been embarrassed, but I knew the truth. There had been nothing I could've done that would have convinced Alpha Waylon to take me.

"Because of your *failure*," he bit out, "you will now serve the gods."

My eyes widened as he crouched down and spoke softly to me through the bars of my cell.

"You will die tonight, Gracie Holloway."

My wolf snapped to attention as he stood and strode out of the prison, the metal door clanging as he slammed it behind him. For the first time, in longer than I could remember, my wolf *howled* in my ears at his blunt words. Die? We would die tonight?

I'd been beaten within an inch of my life before. I'd even wished for death before. But something about Alpha Ivan's threat was unbelievable. I couldn't die. I had just found... What had I just found? Three distinct faces stood out to me in the shadowy depths of my prison.

What was I even thinking? Why was I thinking of

them? Closing my eyes, I wondered how much blood I had lost and why my breathing was still so labored. I should have been healing—most shifters did so efficiently—but my health was so poor that I couldn't even do that properly. The weight of my injuries, of my existence right now, felt almost too much to bear.

Still, there was the *anger*. A kernel of anger was growing inside of me, kindling a flame of rebellion against the notion that Alpha Ivan could just decide to end my life. I'd done everything right. I'd silently endured every second of his abuse, and I was being rewarded with death? With being sacrificed to one of The Eight? My hand curled around the bars of my jail as tears heated my eyes.

Alpha Ivan would—

I stopped myself. I wouldn't call him Alpha Ivan anymore. I had no reason to show him that respect. He didn't deserve it. From now on, even though it would only be in my own head, he would just be Ivan.

Moving back from the bars of my prison, I curled into myself and put my head against my knees. Exhaustion and fear were two sides of the same coin for me right now, and there was no escaping it.

So instead of fighting it, I let my mind wander as I was lulled into a fitful sleep.

. . .

"WHY?" I asked my mom as we stood in the thick crowd of compound members gathered in the arena, the altar before us visible in the torchlight. Nyxarra's statue stood prominently in the center, surrounded by flowers and fruit. The full moon cast a glow on the wooden altar that was already stained a deep red.

"Because we don't have a choice," my mom said softly, reaching out to take my hand. "Don't watch."

Of course, her suggestion wasn't possible—not when horror unfolded in front of me. A teenage girl, maybe fifteen, was dragged before the rest of us and forced to lay on an altar as a priestess spoke through the speakers in the courtyard.

"Tonight we honor the Buck Moon, sacrificing blood on the altar of our goddess to bring blessings to our land."

A gurgle sounded as one of the soldiers slit the girl's throat without any warning, her body going completely limp. No one made a move to help her as she stared up at the sky with dead eyes, blood soaking the altar beneath her.

We'd never worshipped The Eight consistently on our farm. There had been mentions of the gods in passing, but never like this. There could be no light, no blessing that came from this. The priestess continued to speak on it being a holy cleansing, but all it felt like was poison soaking into the land.

Then the shift happened.

A wicked wind moved through our compound, and I watched as Ivan's men shifted violently into their wolves, *fur flashing under the moonlight. Curling against my mother, she tried to soothe me, but the snarls and barks clued me into the erupting violence. It wasn't just the one girl who was being sacrificed; they were pulling people from the crowd. Screams of terror and cries of pain painted the night air.*

I couldn't even pray to The Eight for it to stop, because the gods were why Alpha Ivan had done this.

THERE HAD NEVER BEEN any blessings or miracles that had come from those rituals, and the same would be the case tonight. The rituals only existed to express violence and rage. Ivan enjoyed killing his own people. Ivan loved working them to death, only to sacrifice their loved ones to a god I wasn't sure he even believed in. Tears leaked down my face as I opened my eyes, finding that I'd slipped onto the floor so that I was lying on my side.

My body was still constrained, my ankles heavy with chains. All I could do was lay in the damp, cold jail until Ivan came for me. There were no soldiers in the building, and a singular light hung over a desk across the room. In the dim circle of light it shed, a mouse sprinted from outside the cell to the far corner, as if trying to hide from me.

What could I possibly do to a mouse?

In a different life, I could have been scarier. I could

have had a feral edge like some other wolves have, formed through years of battle. I could have commanded dominance. All of that had been drained from me, submerged under years of pain and suffering. Something I'd forgotten about in the light of meeting...them.

There was no denying it, they'd left an impact on me. Squeezing my eyes shut, I imagined the sensation of Thornar's warm, muscular arms. I could practically feel Basir's inferno stare and Ravik's intense, protective dominance. It almost felt unreal. Like maybe it had all been a dream.

Had they realized yet that I'd been taken? Had they felt the connection that I had? I couldn't have been alone in the intensity of my reaction. There was something there. Something important.

The door of the building opened with a quiet creak.

"Gracie?" Ravina's face appeared at the bars of my cell. I tried to sit up as she looked over me.

"You look like shit, three-one-four."

I let out a pained laugh before sighing. "I...I didn't accomplish what Ivan expected me to. I failed."

Ravina was dressed in our standard cotton dark dress, her hair pulled away from her face with a scarf as she motioned for me to move toward the bars. I breathed a sigh of relief as she began to untie the ropes on my torso.

"I don't want you to get in trouble," I murmured, rubbing my wrists.

"They sent me in here to prepare you before the high priestess arrives—someone from a different compound. They're dressing the altar...I think they plan to sacrifice you."

"Ivan said as much. Waylon refused me. I'm not valuable anymore."

"I don't understand." She frowned, rubbing her head. "I mean, I find you annoying, but didn't they present you to him? That dress you're wearing is expensive..."

Ravina was struggling to put the pieces together, and I figured there was no harm in telling her—especially since Ivan would probably try to do this again with someone else.

"It wasn't me," I breathed out. "He called Ivan out on trafficking shifters. He insulted him publicly. I wasn't even allowed to say anything."

Ravina shook her head sadly. "I really thought you were getting out of here... I guess in some way, you are."

Through death.

Reaching to her bag, sneaking a look at the door, she spoke in a murmur. "They made me search through your belongings, to sort them and give them to others...but I found the pouch from Thalira."

The poison.

Ravina slipped it through the bars and into my hands as I clasped it.

"I can't stay; I know they will come and check on us. But if he's truly going to sacrifice you, beat him to it. Don't let him have that victory. If everything you say is true, he won't let this be a simple offering. He's going to torture you publicly."

The door slammed open, and a guard shouted for her to leave. As quickly as I could, I clasped the pouch and hid it under my legs. I offered Ravina a long look of thanks before she disappeared out of the door, leaving me once again in silence.

Not just silence, but with the weight of decision hanging over me.

Was Ravina right? Would it be better to... I couldn't even finish that thought without my wolf snarling in vicious disagreement. No. It wouldn't be better, would it?

If not me...then someone else.

Maybe I couldn't stop death tonight. But I could decide how it happened.

CHAPTER 11
GRACIE

"IF YOU RUN, YOU DIE. UNDERSTAND?" The soldier was matter-of-fact, either unfeeling or numb to the instructions he delivered. I nodded, walking in front of him from the holding cell and back into the compound yard. I couldn't tell how long I'd been inside that cell, only that the daylight was quickly escaping from the sky. And like a ticking clock, the ritual was fast approaching.

The soldier had instructed me to walk across the yard to the biggest building on the compound, a three-story structure that rose above the rest. The ritual would take place outside, in an arena to the west of the compound. Normally used for training, one night out of each month it became a place of bloodshed and violence.

"Through the door and up the stairs." Another

order, and I didn't hesitate to follow it. The eyes of my fellow pack members—buried in their day of work—were glued to me as I passed. I had no doubt the news of my failure had infiltrated the entire compound. I didn't feel shame, though.

"Last door to your right."

My body ached from climbing the stairs, but I kept going. When I reached the last door to my right, it opened immediately. Velina motioned for me to enter and then closed the door right in the soldier's face.

"Sit."

I stayed silent as I sat in the available chair, keeping my focus on the woman standing in the center of the room.

Throughout my time in the Cold Moon Pack, we'd had several priestesses come and go from the compound—it was routine for a visiting priestess to perform the monthly rituals. But where was Thalira? During monthly rituals she would sit with everyone else after helping to prepare the selected "honored sacrifice." Not this time, though. I hadn't seen or heard a word from her since arriving back. And this woman was very different from any priestess I'd seen before. She wasn't from any of our compounds, or even our territory. There was something distinctly *other* about her and the way she held herself, looking me over with curiosity and objectivity.

"Child of Nyxarra, welcome. My name is Avenyx. I will be preparing you for this sacred execution."

Sacred execution. At least that was a more accurate term than "sacrifice." There would be nothing sacred about it, but at least it was named for what it was—a death penalty.

Her voice was steady and calm, but the look in her eyes was off, and there was nothing to distract from her all-seeing stare. Her white-blonde hair was pulled away from her face in a severe style, and the steel-plated ceremonial armor she wore looked like something out of a novel. Across it lay a black sash bearing Nyxarra's outline, and a large sword hung on her back in a sheath.

Avenyx was terrifying.

"Avenyx is from the temple in the Grimfur Skulk territory. They have an entire academy devoted to being a priestess of Nyxarra," Velina explained. It was the last piece of information I received before Avenyx motioned for me to stand.

I was stripped of my dress, left in practically nothing, my body trembling at the stark reminder of how little control I had here. My ankles were still weighed down by chains, and as Avenyx and Velina began to scrub my skin with a rough sponge and cold water, I let my eyes fall shut. The moment felt violating, somehow more than others I'd been through recently.

Only when Velina pulled a cotton dress over my head did I feel better.

My skin was raw, and I winced as Avenyx began to paint my body in ceremonial patterns I'd never seen before. Something was different about tonight's ritual —that much was obvious. I just didn't understand what. The only thing I could appreciate was that Avenyx wasn't cruel in her actions. She was simply being meticulous in her process, especially while decorating my skin.

My nose twitched at the metallic scent of the paint, and I began to feel lightheaded.

When Avenyx chanted in quiet tones, Velina took a step back and began to straighten the room. Her part in this ritual was over. Sage and lavender wafted over me as Avenyx's words floated to my ears.

"This death is sacred; it will fuel the goddess's command. Nyxarra, your soldier sacrifices her life tonight, willingly and joyfully." Tears crowded my eyes, and I looked up at the ceiling as I tried to blink them away. "Your child has failed her mortal duties, but she will serve you in the Vast as she passes from this realm to the next."

The Vast...would I truly go there? I hadn't allowed my thoughts to go that far. *From the Vast we are born; to the Vast we return.* I'd heard that often in my life. I'd be overjoyed to reunite with Mom and Dad, but what about Owen? Who'd be left to find him?

Avenyx's fingers traced over the center of my chest, causing a pulse of pain as she painted over the bruise from Ivan's heavy boot.

"Don't be afraid, child. Nyxarra welcomes you to the Vast."

It was too much. I wasn't sure how much longer my feet would support me. I was only saved by her exit, leaving me with Velina, who watched from the corner in silence. I gasped as the door thudded closed, unable to keep the panic at bay.

This was really going to happen. I was going to die.

My wolf was silent. I didn't understand the markings on my body, but I knew what they did. They'd wrapped my wolf in chains. She couldn't move; she couldn't howl. We were prisoners of our bleak and very short future.

"I'll pretend I didn't find this on you." Velina pinched a vial between her thumb and forefinger. The poison.

"I wouldn't use it," I murmured, then tried to move past my terror and strengthen my resolve. "If not me... someone else."

Velina's laugh was sharp and cruel. "You worry about others on the edge of your own death? We're all damned under the Cold Moon Pack."

I nodded, not disagreeing with her. Knowing I wouldn't speak with her again after this, I found myself asking, "Why? Why do you stand by his side? How long have you stood by his side?"

Velina's gaze turned distant as she stared at the door behind me, her answer revealing more than I could have ever expected. "Since the day he was born."

My eyes widened. "You're related to Ivan?"

"Alpha Ivan," she snapped, but I didn't correct myself. "But yes, I'm his sister." Before I could ask her anything else, she was standing at the door. "They'll come for you in a few minutes. Prepare yourself."

Once again, I was left in silence to consider what I'd just learned. Ivan had a sister. I suppose that wasn't surprising, but it did show the extent of his cruelty. If he treated his own sister that way, what hope was there for the rest of us?

"Three-one-four. Stand."

The same soldier had come for me, and I didn't bother correcting him on the number. Somehow it bothered me less than if he'd called me Gracie. I stood and watched as he unlocked the chain at my ankles, then grabbed hold of my arm and marched me toward the door.

As the two of us walked forward, armed men joined to either side of us as an escort. The sound of boots against the ground and the clink of their guns against their vests cemented the fact that this was a death march. When we turned to make our way toward the arena, I raised my eyes to look around.

Over a hundred workers had stopped in their tracks, watching the procession. They'd probably follow behind to witness the rest of the mandatory "celebration."

Gas-lit torches lined our path, the autumnal sky darkening into night. A banner featuring Nyxarra hung prominently over the arena's entrance, strung between the sniper towers on either end. All of Ivan's men were gathered, and workers were being ushered into the stands on the far side of the arena. I wouldn't be facing them, though. I would be facing Ivan, who would sit front and center like a king.

Most of this was familiar, like every month on the full moon. But the center of the arena didn't hold the usual wooden altar and bounty. Instead, Avenyx stood in front of a marble slab raised four inches off the ground, surrounded by skulls. Smoke wafted from them, and the scent of rot permeated the air.

The beating of drums was heavy in my ears as I took the last few steps to her altar.

"Join me at the table of offerings." She motioned to the slab. As the guard released me, she took my hand, helping me sit on the stone. Everything about the moment felt surreal, and as Avenyx worked, spreading tools out in front of her, I watched absently as the arena continued to fill. Quiet conversations and murmurs spread throughout, and armed soldiers formed a perimeter around the altar.

Did they truly think I would try to escape? I knew I would be gunned down without a thought.

"What a beautiful night to be offered," Avenyx murmured. "Clear sky, showing off the Buck Moon. Nyxarra blesses her soldiers."

She was right—it was a beautiful, clear night. The smoke curling around me made the stars seem fuzzy as I watched them twinkle brightly. A small smile tugged at my lips as I imagined Basir, Ravik, and Thornar seeing the same sky.

Surely, as wolves, they would enjoy it just as much.

It was foolish. Madness. But a small part of me wished—maybe hoped—that I could see them once before it all ended.

CHAPTER 12
THORNAR

THE SPARK in my chest that Gracie had lit was now a full-blown firestorm. The heat scorched my heart, and my gaze—though fixed on the outside world—was shaded by her. My wolf let out a savage snarl in my head, demanding we move faster.

The blades of the helicopter thundered, and I was left to my own thoughts as I perched in the open door, watching the terrain of Iridale blur beneath us. Silverpine, the country north of Thornfell, had granted us clearance to cross their borders, and our jet had flown straight from Scarlet Sloth territory to one of their military airstrips.

Once the Silverpine officials learned our objective —to infiltrate Ivan's compound, tucked just beyond the border in the northeast corner of Thornfell— they'd happily given us a corridor and wished us luck.

No one fucking liked Ivan, but until now, no one had been ready to stand up to him, either.

And we hadn't lied to them about the plan. We did plan on extracting information on what the hell he was doing behind those high compound walls. But more importantly, we were here to pull my little flame out of the bleak, sterile hell that was the Cold Moon Pack.

It was a driving, almost insatiable need to have her in my arms again. To prove to her that she didn't need to live in fear—that she didn't need to flinch. That an existence outside that kind of terror was possible. It might've taken me and my sister years to learn that, but I liked to think I turned out fine.

"Deegan is going to kill us," I said to Ravik through the mic in my helmet, his gaze locked on the ground below. Basir had his eyes shut like he was sleeping, but I didn't buy that shit for a second.

I usually didn't give a damn about other people's opinions, but Deegan's? That was different. Since I'd come to the Ironsun Pack, he'd become more than a mentor—he was like a father to me. Not by blood, but it didn't matter. Normally we'd wait for permission before pulling off something like this, but with him currently indisposed, none of us were willing to sit still.

Every second we wasted was a second Gracie could be—

"He'll understand. Especially if we bring back extra information," Ravik said. "I already briefed the other two groups—to grab anyone who looks like they want out. It'll be easier to get intel from people willing to talk."

Call me crazy, but I had a feeling there'd be a lot of people who wanted out of Ivan's grip. The bastard was known for mistreating his people—hell, he fucking bragged about it.

"Deegan didn't kill us for that mission in Goldmere," Basir pointed out.

I chuckled. I mean...he wasn't wrong, but Goldmere wasn't Thornfell. The politics and interests in the continent south of us were far more discreet.

My eyes closed as I remembered the bruises that covered Gracie's body, the blood soaking her ivory dress when I found her in that emergency stairwell. I'd instantly clocked how bad she was hurt, unable to stop myself from moving closer. Like a moth to flame, completely mesmerized by the way her eyes lit up when she saw me. A wounded creature energized by hope.

My heart had erupted in flames the moment I laid eyes on her.

Unexpected, but completely fucking welcome. This wasn't recklessness, not this time. It was instinct. Necessary. The second we realized she'd been stolen from us, there was only one thing left to do. *Bring her back.*

"Five minutes until we're within range of North-grove," the pilot announced, and I reached across my chest to do one last check of the buckles on my parachute. Our team was dressed in black tactical gear and strapped with as many weapons as possible—something that made me feel confident we could pull this off.

It would be a HALO jump, and we would have to land perfectly within the confines of the camp without drawing attention. We'd already determined that the arena within the compound would be a good place to do so, allowing us to infiltrate the base silently.

There were thirty of us in total. One of the helicopters would be in charge of landing outside the walls and detonating a piece of the compound's border to create an escape route. All we had to do was get her through the wall and onto one of those helicopters, and then we would get the fuck out of here.

This wasn't the first time that the three of us had done dangerous shit like this. In fact, I tended to make a habit of it—although it was never for a reason like Gracie. I just liked to think that I took really fucking well to training. Not to mention, I was fantastic with a gun and explosives.

"This could all go to shit!" I warned, though I didn't know why. It wasn't like I was going to change anyone's mind, even my own. Basir nodded. It was more than likely we wouldn't walk out of this unharmed, but it would be worth it if Gracie woke up in our territory tomorrow.

It had been less than twenty-four hours since I'd last seen her, and now I was traveling across Thornfell to get her back.

We were totally fucked.

"At least it's better than sitting through the trade council." I barked out a laugh. Ravik wasn't wrong. The TTC had been dry and dull, and considering we had deals with every territory except Ivan's, completely unnecessary.

Gracie mattered far more than any of that shit.

"There it is!" I called out, feeling a surge of adrenaline as I stood, gripping the handle next to me. The terrain had been slowly becoming more barren since leaving Silverpine, but now I could almost go as far as to say it appeared hostile.

Dead, ashy lands lay below us in the dark, my wolf tracking every inch of it. There was absolutely no life. No vegetation. No animals.

There was an eerie silence over the land, and while I knew our helicopters were loud to me, I knew just how silently they moved through the air above.

"That's where she's been living?" Ravik demanded, looking at the approaching compound. My jaw clenched in anger, because the state of the compound was dire.

Fog hung from the sniper towers positioned incrementally along the barbed wire fences, making it clear that outsiders weren't welcome. Fluorescent floodlights blasted across the grounds, illuminating the rusted metal shacks that served as buildings for those who lived here. The compound wasn't particularly large, but it had a central living space, an arena, and a sizable training center. Soldiers stood guard at the perimeter of Northgrove, strapped with guns and staring out into the vast, barren territory ahead of them.

I had heard the rumors in the past of sacrificial rituals and trafficking shifters. I'd heard about the cruelty of the Cold Moon Pack. But to see the truth?

I'd never felt such fury.

Gracie had been living like this, presumably for her entire life.

"Shit, they're using the arena," Basir said.

A sense of dread permeated the air. That many people didn't gather on their own or for sport.

They gathered like that for blood.

"Drop us above the central compound," I told the pilot, "but tell the other teams to blow open a section of the wall near the arena. I have a feeling that's where we're going to find our girl."

After receiving an affirmative, we got into ready

positions. When the helicopters moved silently over the empty central space of the compound, I jumped. I had never been one to hesitate, and it sure as fuck wouldn't start now.

The wind was cold and tasted bitter as I fell through the air, silently pulling to release the parachute. With a tug upward I slowed, drifting down into the shadows of a large building that appeared to be a house. My wolf surged forward as I shed the parachute, somehow managing to keep him in his cage. It wasn't time for that—not yet. Not until we had eyes on Gracie.

I could smell her vanilla and cinnamon scent. It was everywhere.

It was also tinged with blood.

When my pack brothers landed, we moved quietly, staying in the shadows as we weaved through the dilapidated buildings. I could feel the tension in Ravik as he tried to contain his wolf, having caught her scent as well. And Basir, while silent, continuously played with the knife he always carried. It was a sign that his facade of calm was fractured, close to breaking, which wouldn't be good for anyone.

I didn't hide the violence inside of me, allowing it to break out—especially if it meant protecting those I cared about. I knew Ravik felt the same. Basir, though, was a different situation, and it was probably best that he didn't lose his shit. After all, there was a reason he was an Enforcer.

Ravik motioned for a change in our trajectory, and I nodded sharply. Tonight, the full moon shone brightly down on the compound, leaving little room for mistakes—but it was clear that everyone was at the arena. Luckily, because of the mass of people, they wouldn't notice the shift in power from our arrival, even if each of us carried the distinct dominance and presence that came with being an alpha.

A sense of warning began to grow as we moved beneath the stands of the arena, trying to get a gauge on the space as a whole. How the hell would we find her...

My heart stopped in my chest.

At the center of the arena, amidst haunting ceremonial drums and the scent of sage, Gracie lay on a marble slab. Blood rushed in my ears, and my wolf began to break free, forcing a grunt of pain from my chest as I barely managed to hold him back. Ravik was saying something, but I couldn't hear him. I couldn't hear anything.

All I could focus on was Gracie, laid out on an altar and surrounded by skulls. Her slight frame was draped in a barely-there dress, ritual paint scrawled across her exposed skin. They'd dressed her up like a corpse, as if she was already gone. But she wasn't. *Not yet.*

The woman standing over her chanted melodically as my little flame trembled. What the fuck was going on?

Then she picked up a ceremonial knife, holding it high in the air as if presenting it to The Eight. A snarl ripped from my throat. They were going to sacrifice her to their gods. Discard her as if she wasn't the most sacred thing we'd ever seen.

I didn't understand why, or if it was just punishment, but...they were going to kill her.

"We need to pull her out of there, now. Consequences be damned," I bit out.

"It won't help her if we're shot," Basir hissed, his fury finally breaking through.

"It doesn't matter—we have to get her," Ravik said, his voice hard but level. "I'm calling in the other team. I'll have them detonate the far wall where there aren't any people. The distraction should give us enough time to grab her."

Before we could say another word, the drums stopped. The speaker system crackled to life, the expectant silence of the crowd making it feel as if the arena itself was holding its breath. A voice filled with disdain flooded the space, echoing through the compound.

"On this holy night of the Buck Moon, please welcome your esteemed Alpha, Ivan Rivers."

He was about to sacrifice her himself.

And we were about to bring down the walls of Gracie's prison.

CHAPTER 13
GRACIE

MY EYES FELT heavy as the smoke curling around me thickened, sweet and sharp like overripe fruit. My brain blurred at the edges, my thoughts growing slow and sludgy. Was this normal for rituals?

"Breathe in the smoke. It will help you connect to Nyxarra." Avenyx confirmed it: they wanted me drugged so I'd look willing.

Despite knowing their intention, I didn't stop the smoke from invading my lungs as she began to chant softly. My eyes fell shut, and I could feel the arena growing more and more crowded, everyone coming to witness my unexpected death.

I just had to hope the children wouldn't be brought to this. They didn't deserve those nightmares. No one did.

Suddenly, underneath the haze of smoke, something sparked. My ears rang. My chest warmed. My heavy eyes opened. I sensed something different in the air, but my body was so lethargic I couldn't move. Managing to turn my head toward Avenyx, I noticed she had laid out a cloth on a small table in front of her, four knives gleaming on top.

Whatever had pulled my attention before was nothing compared to the sharp edges of steel that would soon tear open my flesh. A tremble overtook me. I tried not to show my fear, but I couldn't help the tears that welled in my eyes. I couldn't move. I could only *experience* as gazes fell on me from every direction.

What upset me more, though, was what I *couldn't* feel. Whatever had sparked that warmth in my chest a moment ago was gone, as if I'd imagined it. It had reminded me so much of the three men I'd met at the conference, the reactions they'd evoked in both me and my wolf. Maybe it was my brain's way of coping—pulling forward a pleasant memory to distract me from the horror of the present.

I remembered how they'd felt when they touched me. Basir. Ravik. Thornar.

Their names played a soft, distracting song in my head—interrupted by the sudden crackling of the loudspeakers and the ceasing of the drums. It was nearly time.

Velina's voice filled the air. "On this holy night of

the Buck Moon, please welcome your esteemed Alpha, Ivan Rivers."

The arena filled with cheers, a roar of applause that felt panicked. Everyone knew what would happen if they didn't support Ivan's need to be worshiped. He would rather set this arena on fire than suffer such an insult.

Ivan took the microphone. "Tonight we honor the Buck Moon, sacrificing one of our own in honor of our goddess." I might have grimaced, if I'd been able to control my body. *One of our own?* What a convenient time for him to decide I belonged. Ivan had never sacrificed one of his men—only innocents stuck in his prison.

"Once every full moon, we cleanse these lands. We sacrifice the weak to make room for the strong." Ivan's voice was sharp, cruel, filled with loathing toward me. "Tonight's sacrifice shows all of us that even those given the greatest of chances will fail if they are weak. So we remove the dirt, the trash plaguing our lands, to make room for the future."

He raged about control being preserved and blood-lines being pure, bleeding out the chaos. His words were a blade meant to degrade, but they barely touched me.

All I could focus on was the ceremonial cloth beneath Avenyx's knives and the way the gods stared back.

Astaruun, the creator of life.
Nyxarra, the mother of shadows and moonlight.
Vorrakar, the father of illumination and sunlight.
Thaloryn, the father of depth and waves.
Sylvaern, the mother of growth and roots.
Yvelis, the god of transitions and bone.

There were two others, but they were only represented by wisps of smoke. No names. No faces. Just shadows where gods should've been. We were taught to worship The Eight, but no one ever talked about those two. Like they'd been erased. Or maybe hidden.

Some whispered that one was the god of creatures, wild and untamed. Others claimed they were gods of chaos, banished by Astaruun for something too dark to speak of.

I didn't know what to believe. But staring at those empty spaces on the cloth, I couldn't help but wonder...what did they do to be forgotten? Or worse—what if they hadn't been forgotten at all?

"...and this is why we sacrifice to Nyxarra—to bring blessings to our territory!"

Ivan's voice broke through my thoughts as the name Nyxarra vibrated the air around us. Pain pulsed through my head as the smoke thickened, the scent of rot and ozone filling my nose. My chest squeezed; I could barely breathe. A wheeze came from my lips, but I couldn't move. *Something was wrong.* I may not have been a priestess of The Eight, but I could feel the corruption in the air. Nothing about this was natural.

Ivan's voice became distorted in the background as the world turned gray, a shadow of the world that had existed seconds before. I could see, past the high priestess, a sobbing woman on the ground. She was clothed in black, and the tears that fell from her eyes shimmered like moonlight. Her wrists were bound in shackles, just like mine.

The earth shifted underneath us, rattling the arena, and her gaze snapped up, her features painted in panic as a shadow eclipsed her. I could feel her terror. I could sense the malice radiating from the shadow. The power it wielded to imprison her was immense.

Only once the shadow had passed did relief color the woman's face. But then her sobs continued, making my chest ache with her pain. I tried to move off the altar to get to her, and when she looked up again, silver tears stained her face. Not wrathful. Just...devastated.

"This is not my will," she whispered. Then again, louder. Until the world cracked at the seams. "This is not my will!"

Her scream blew out my eardrums and threw me from the hallucination as I felt hot blood leak down my jaw. My eyes snapped open to see Avenyx driving a knife down toward my chest.

In that second, everything changed.

Pain lashed across my torso and a scream ripped from my throat, my back arching off the marble that exploded with a blaze of heat. Somewhere, something detonated. The sound of an explosion, much like that night at the farm, rang through the air. Avenyx was thrown backward, the knife clattering to the marble altar.

A wall of smoke and dark magic rose up around me, bursting from the altar and slamming everything and everyone in its path to the ground. I screamed as power surged through me like lightning, and that voice—the cry of the sobbing woman—seemed to imprint itself on my very soul.

The ritual had been stopped—broken—and it had left a mark.

"The west wall has been destroyed!"

I heard the words distantly as savage growls and howls filled the air. I managed to push myself up, barely able to see two feet in front of me. But what I did see was pure chaos.

Gunfire cracked, causing my ears to pulse in pain, and I could taste blood. People screamed as they threw themselves out of the stands to escape the force crashing through the west wall. Black uniforms carrying guns swept inside, and above us, helicopter lights shone down on the center of the compound.

My wolf slammed up into my chest, propelling us

forward and off the marble—the painted chains that had laid heavily on our skin no longer holding us captive. I crawled away from it, trying to heed her plea to take my chance—to escape. I stumbled to my feet, legs weak and shaking, my gaze fixed on the exit that had been blown open.

"No, you don't, girl." Ivan's hand wrapped in my hair and pulled me back hard. I cried out, and before he could drag me further, he was intercepted, tackled by one of the largest wolves I'd ever seen. The wolf was white, almost like snow, with gold eyes and massive teeth snapping at Ivan's neck.

"No!" When a shot rang out, hitting the ground near the wolf, I surged forward, trying to protect it. Luckily, in that moment, the wolf darted away and sprinted toward me. My eyes welled with tears as I wrapped my arms around my savior.

I recognized its power, but everything was so hazy I couldn't fully piece together who they were. When another wolf joined us—a sleek, onyx-colored one—I breathed a sigh of relief. A feeling of protection bloomed in me. We had to get out, though. We couldn't dodge Ivan's men forever.

"*Lux mea.*" Ravik's voice cut through everything else as I found him crouched in front of me, his gaze filled with so much depth...so much affection.

I didn't hold back. Throwing myself into his arms, he stood, and I could see both wolves clearing the way forward. Was it possible that those were Basir and Thornar? I tried to breathe through the pain wrecking my body as tears began to streak down my face.

"Were you shot? Did she get you with that damn knife?" Ravik demanded, panic and urgency layered in his voice.

"It's the ritual. It didn't finish, and I had this vision..." My eyes grew heavy as I felt something roll over me.

It was primordial. It tasted like blood on my tongue, and a dark power, much like the one that had exploded from the altar, began to push out of my chest. Seizing in Ravik's arms, black smoke poured from my mouth, a thick cloud surrounding the four of us.

Echoes of chants and the sensation of hands skimming my skin made me shake in fear. In front of me appeared a face—not Ravik or either of the wolves—but *her*. The woman. The goddess. Nyxarra. Drumbeats swelled until my ears ached from the pressure, and she reached forward, pressing a finger to the center of my chest.

My world exploded in searing pain as power lashed through me.

A tight connection snapped into place between me and my rescuers, raw and ancient. Not just mates. Not just magic. Something so much more...something divine.

Ravik stumbled from the force of it, clasping me tighter to his chest as the other two shifted back on either side of us.

"Fuck!" Thornar's voice was raw and filled with pain, but it was drowned out by Nyxarra.

"You've freed me, child of shadows and moonlight."

Those words blanketed me in darkness, the sounds of battle disappearing—and before I could say another word, the Vast collapsed over me.

CHAPTER 14
GRACIE

A CRACK of lightning split the air, and then a wave of darkness crashed over me. I sank into its depths, weightless and consumed—until a warm glow began to rise from my chest, soft and steady. Calling me forward. Reminding me of...something.

My eyes felt heavy as I tried to pry them open, feeling as though my skin was cocooned in clouds. Soft silk drifted against me as I slid my fingers across the plush surface underneath me, the unfamiliar territory forcing me to wake up.

Despite the strange location, I wasn't scared. I couldn't remember yet how I'd come here, but I felt safe. Or as safe as I could feel after everything I'd experienced.

That thought was like gasoline to a flame. My eyes snapped open. A whoosh of air left my chest, and my body trembled with the aftershocks of what should have been a terrible nightmare. I'd nearly died. I'd nearly been sacrificed to Nyxarra.

The goddess's tear-streaked face flashed before me in the dark room as I slowly brought myself to sit. It felt far more difficult to breathe than normal, and there was an ache in my bones.

As my eyes adjusted to the darkness of the room, though, my physical state was long forgotten. Awe cascaded over me as my gaze trailed across the luxu-rious cream-colored bedding that surrounded me like a vast sea, to the expansive room that seemed to go on forever in each direction, except behind me. The details were muted, but the firelight from the sitting area to my left highlighted a bookcase filled with heavy, leather-bound texts. Further in that direction of the room lay a wall of curtains, the faintest ray of daylight breaking through the center.

Where was I? How did I get here? The last thing I remembered was...Ravik? And two dangerous wolves by our side as he carried me out of the compound. Nothing else existed between that point and now, and the void was starting to make me uneasy.

Had they truly come for me? Had we managed to escape? Or had we died—had their attempt to save me resulted in all of our deaths? Hot tears welled in my eyes as I looked down at my bare arms, finding that they were free from bruises or scars. The paint from the ceremony had been washed off, and my skin seemed to sparkle in the dim lighting. Even my fingers looked healed as I brought them up to my hair, finding it feather-soft to the touch.

Inside of me, my wolf slept silently, a soft purr leaving her chest.

We'd died. There was no other possible explanation for being in a place like this and for feeling so... amazing. *Whole*. I was tired and achy, sure, but my head felt clear for the first time in a long time, and my stomach didn't ache with hunger. A whimper left my throat as I shifted toward the edge of the gigantic bed, a thin-strapped gown drifting around my frame.

Maybe if I opened those heavy curtains, I'd have a better understanding of where I was and how I'd gotten here. The plush carpet beneath my toes was a welcome surprise as I moved silently across the room, my progress slowed by the flowers that littered the room in vases. I paused at each one along my path, taking time to stroke their petals and leaves. Whenever we'd had flowers in the compound, they were placed off-limits in the shrine. So being able to not only touch but smell them felt like a luxury.

I parted through the wall of curtains, finding the handle on the door behind them. Giving it a good tug to the right, it slid open effortlessly, and a brilliant flash of sunlight filled the room like an eruption of flames. My hand covered my eyes as I squinted, trying to adjust to the drastic change before stepping out over the threshold.

"By the gods..." My voice was hoarse as I froze, captured in place by...*paradise.*

The sunlit sky was a stunning sapphire, hanging with frosted clouds that shimmered with streaks of lavender and teal. Silver mist filled the air, the sensation of it seeping into my lungs bringing chills to my skin, a direct contrast to the warmth of the sun hanging in the sky. Massive mountains with fog curled around them lay in the distance, their tips tinged in a soft gold that stood sentinel over the city.

There was a hum of power in the air, and below I could see and hear the bustling metropolis waking up for the day. It was painful how beautiful and clean the land was, making me feel uncomfortable compared to the brutal state of the compound. Yet at the same time, it felt right. It felt like the land was blessed and that I was being welcomed into it.

I turned to look back at the building I'd emerged from, the stone balcony extending from a glass wall that allowed for a grand view of the territory. Over the glass railing hung a flag with a familiar red and gold crest. This was Ironsun Pack territory.

I hadn't died. I'd truly been saved.

My legs felt wobbly, my head filled with a buoyancy that I recognized. My hands gripped the wall in front of me as spots filled my vision. It was all too much, a dream come true. How could I trust myself? How could I trust my eyes? Nothing this good had—

A warm, muscular arm locked around my waist while another caught my knees, lifting me into a bridal hold. A surge of familiar magic rolled over me, tugging on that bond buried deep within my chest, my head shooting up to see...Basir.

The last time I'd seen him had been filled with pain and panic. Now, though, none of that existed. I was completely captivated by his scent, by everything about him. Never before had I felt such an intense reaction to anyone, except for Ravik and Thornar. It made my stomach twist nervously and a flush roll up my cheeks. I didn't understand the sensation coiling around me and why the rumble from his chest only made it worse.

Of course, I knew about mating and the sensation you were supposed to feel, but having lived so long in fear and then to feel...this. It was dizzying. Intoxicating.

My voice broke the silence between us. "You're here."

He stared down into my expression, his grip tightening at the sound of my voice. I shivered at the feeling as he grunted, moving across the balcony to a table and chairs. I felt a surge of disappointment as he gently placed me down.

Basir moved across the balcony as quickly as he'd appeared.

"I didn't mean it as a bad thing," I tried to explain, pressing a hand to my chest to try and calm my anxiety. "I just didn't expect it. I don't remember much after the compound."

A deep vibration rolled from Basir's chest as he stared down at the city, allowing me a moment to stare at him. His hair was loose, freshly washed and hanging around his shoulders. His military gear was gone, and now he wore a black linen shirt and dark pants and boots. He seemed to exist as a shadow right on the periphery, always there, even when I didn't fully expect it.

"We pulled you out of there," he said quietly. "You were flown to Ironsun Pack territory and placed in a medically induced coma to help you heal."

I swallowed, shame prickling beneath my skin at the thought of the state they'd found me in. "I didn't realize my injuries were that bad."

"You were seizing after you blacked out, though they couldn't figure out why. You were severely malnourished and dehydrated. They got you on fluids quickly. Once your vitals stabilized, your wolf took over." He hesitated for a beat. "It's been five days."

He'd delivered the information so clinically, but there was something underneath his words, and his own commentary brought him to clenching the glass so hard his knuckles turned white. He seemed angry about my state.

"I didn't mean to inconvenience anyone—"

Basir appeared in front of me like a phantom disappearing and reappearing, making me sway in my seat. He crouched down, overwhelming me with the intensity of emotion on his face. I couldn't put a name to the emotion because I'd never seen it before, which is probably why it made me do something uncharacteristically bold.

I reached out to touch his chest. It felt like it was necessary, especially with him so close. Immediately, Basir's gaze snapped down to where my fingers grazed him, and he let out a low rumble. *Why did that sound make my heart flutter like this?*

I pulled my hand back. "I shouldn't have touched you without you saying—"

Basir's hand clasped around mine, placing it back on his chest. "You can touch me." The words floated between us, and while they were simple enough, he seemed surprised he'd said them. "You didn't inconvenience anyone, Gracie. You were at Yvelis's door."

The god of death.

The connection between us hummed with pleasure, and I found myself wanting to ask him about it— to see if he could feel it as well. Instead, I managed the next best question.

"The three of you saved me..." I let that hang there,

his gaze never moving. His lips never parting to deny it. "Won't this be considered an open attack on the Cold Moon Pack?"

"Possibly. But we were able to extract others as well. Even if Ivan wants to retaliate, the other territories haven't opposed our actions—mostly because of the intel we've gained."

Disappointment bloomed deep in my chest. I couldn't pinpoint the reason at first, but the truth hit hard, cold, and sudden.

Had they only saved me for the intel I could provide?

Was I just a convenient catalyst for a military operation?

My throat tightened as my wolf shifted inside me, uneasy. Discontent curled through our bond like smoke. I shouldn't have felt this way. I should have felt thankful and grateful I'd been saved. But my wolf and I had wanted something more. We'd wanted him to see it, feel it.

I hadn't imagined the connection between us. But maybe Basir didn't want the connection.

"Right," I whispered, my voice dipping in confidence. "Well, thank you. No matter your reason, you've saved me from death. I can never thank any of you enough."

"You don't need to thank us." Basir's voice was

filled with caution. He could tell something was wrong.

Of course, at that exact moment—before I could explain—my stomach rumbled. Loudly. My cheeks burst into flames as I ducked my head. A momentary sense of shame mixed with fear rolled over me. Showing hunger in the Cold Moon Pack was nearly forbidden.

"You need to eat," Basir said sharply, pulling me up and out of the chair before stepping back once more. He strode inside, sorting through something behind a door to the left of the space. Nibbling my lip, I looked around the sunlit bedroom.

It was easily the size of the first floor of Ivan's home. Blown glass sconces dotted wallpapered walls, the entire space filled with warm golds and creams. It was refined luxury, and the soft scent of vanilla infused the room.

"Whose room is this?" I called out cautiously.

"Yours."

I frowned. "Is it a spare? I don't want to—"

"It's yours." Basir said, his voice harder as he stepped out of the closet. "Yours, Gracie. No strings attached, just your own space."

Something about his sure and direct words had me breathing out a sigh of relief. There was no question about his meaning. This was *my* room. *By the gods.* Tightness in my chest expanded up to my throat as I tried to breathe through it. This type of luxury wasn't something I would ever grow used to, and being told that it belonged to me... I nearly felt sick to my stomach.

"The boxes have been unpacked, and your bags are spread out," Basir said as he stepped out of the closet, motioning toward the space. "Take your time. Wear whatever makes you comfortable."

His gaze lingered for a beat before he added, "There's a bite to the air this morning, so dress warm." Then, softer, almost like an offering, he said, "When you're ready, come outside. I'm taking you to breakfast."

"Of course." I nodded immediately. "Thank you, Basir."

The way he stared at me for a long moment had my heart beating in my chest, fast and hard, before he turned for the door. The sound of the click, signifying his departure, sent a breath tumbling out of me as I sank into the carpet.

It was overwhelming, but I couldn't look away from this fortune. I had a chance to start over, to actually *live*. I wouldn't deny myself that.

CHAPTER 15
GRACIE

IF I HADN'T FELT out of my comfort zone before, I certainly did now.

My gaze was riveted on my reflection, unsure if I was ready to face the day outside these doors. I wouldn't have judged myself too harshly for wanting to stay hidden behind them...but Basir was waiting.

What would he think of how I looked?

There had been piles of clothes to choose from, all newly bought, and I'd made it through half of them before deciding what to wear. It hadn't been easy. I didn't even know what size I was anymore, and I was thankful that whoever had purchased these had guessed correctly.

But they couldn't really be just for me, right? Basir said they'd rescued others, too, so surely these were meant to share.

A fitted cream-colored wrap sweater made of a material called cashmere wrapped around my torso, the long sleeves brushing over my palms. The threading at the edges was gold, with small moons that matched the belt cinched at my waist. My legs were covered in high-waisted dark gray pants that tapered down to my ankles and tucked into my socks to keep me warm. Paired with flat, lace-up black leather ankle boots, I felt cozy and ready for the day.

I also felt like I was wearing clothes far too expensive for someone like me. My hair was loosely braided to the side with a leather tie, and I searched the mirror for something familiar. There was a faint echo of the girl I remembered from before the raids.

I could find it in the necklace and two rings my mother had left me—simple gold bands, one hanging as a pendant at my throat, set with a small amber stone that caught the light. I was glad, at least, that they were safe. When I'd been ripped away from the hotel room, I was sure I'd lost them forever. But Basir had brought them back to me, and that meant more than I could properly express to him.

It wasn't enough to be comforting, though, and I had a feeling that I would need to find myself—a version of myself that was no longer a prisoner. It was a notion that seemed impossible to consider.

Smoothing my fingers through the end of my braid, I marvelled at just how soft it was. I hadn't even needed a shower. My skin and hair were already clean, freshly washed by someone else while I'd been unconscious.

Finally, slipping on a deep green coat that fell to the middle of my thigh, I took a deep breath and turned to face the door. My hand wrapped around the handle. I refused to give myself more than a second to think about this. I couldn't hide from whatever waited for me out there. If I did, it would spit in the face of anyone who sacrificed their life breaking into the compound.

I didn't know if I was ready.

But I was going to do my best to try to live again.

The door opened with a soft whoosh. I squinted, direct sunlight beaming through a hallway window. The cream-colored corridor was quiet and empty as I made my way past several windows, all peering down on the city. I'd never been in a building so tall or large, and I hoped that Basir wasn't far away and that I wouldn't have to search for him. My world had been so small for so long, the idea of trying to find him was intimidating.

The corridor led to a circular foyer with a domed glass ceiling, the bright blue skies making the marble floor glitter like diamonds were embedded within. Three hallways led from the foyer all going in different directions. The one opposite mine led to a series of closed doors that I had to assume were bedrooms, but the central one had a long skylight window that ran the length of the hallway until it opened up into a much larger living space. Making my way slowly toward it, I was caught off guard by the beautiful scene in front of me, my eyes absorbing every element of the opulent yet understated luxury that these men lived in—assuming this was their house.

I wouldn't think about how happy it made me to be in their house in the first place.

A floor-to-ceiling glass wall stood across the space, and between me and it were gorgeous pieces of polished wood furniture and soft, cozy sitting areas, all accented by rugs that made the space feel soft and warm. Hesitating at the doorway, I looked around for Basir but didn't see him anywhere, my brow dipping in confusion.

The door behind me in the foyer clicked open. I turned sharply, feeling a surge of panic at the surprise. Nothing good ever came of surprises.

Basir stood in the entrance, fresh air from outside drifting in as he looked at me in concern. "Are you okay?"

"Am I okay?" I asked softly, making my way toward him.

"I felt—" Basir cut himself off and shook his head, my heart racing. He had felt *what? I needed to know.* It was the closest I'd gotten to confirming our connection. "Come on, glow, let's get you food."

"Glow?" Basir may have been looking right at me, only inches away, but he was throwing walls up between us. I could almost feel his trepidation, as if he hadn't meant to confirm our connection or call me glow.

"Yeah, glow," he confirmed, running a hand through his hair.

"Why glow?" I asked seriously.

"Your hair." His answer was immediate. "It reminds me of...it doesn't matter. Come on."

With a gentle tug of my hand, Basir led me through the door and into the open-air hallway. A smile tugged at my lips, and I pulled him to a stop, unable to help myself.

"I...like it. I like glow. You can call me that." My voice was barely a whisper, a nervous energy invading my chest. I couldn't ask him to confirm our connection, fearing rejection, but the nickname? I could tell him I liked that.

I couldn't even begin to express how good it felt to *give* my opinion on something without fear.

Basir's emerald gaze deepened and the gold streaks within seemed to grow brighter, his fingers tightening in mine before he offered a single nod. I didn't mind when he led us forward this time, because even with the awkwardness between us, it felt like he *might* understand what I was feeling and trying to express. Maybe I should have felt uncomfortable holding his hand, but I didn't.

"This is a huge building," I whispered, looking up at the top floor we'd just left.

The building had to have at least thirty floors, and while it appeared to be square, the center of it was open all the way to the bottom, with staircases and elevators leading to each level. The top three floors seemed to have less access points, and considering we were coming from the very top, it was pretty easy to see how few people there were up here compared to the bottom.

"It's more of a castle," Basir admitted roughly. "Although it took a while before I could think of it like that without feeling..."

"Overwhelmed?"

He gave a sharp nod, and I felt a sense of accomplishment that I'd been able to understand his feelings. I squeezed his hand as we reached the second-highest floor. I understood what he meant about it being a castle. While it looked like a skyscraper, there was an air of majesty to it that couldn't be denied. Glass, steel, and stone covered every surface, and the open air made the Ironsun Pack flags shift in the wind in flashes of red and gold. The furniture that decorated even the open corridor was finely crafted and luxurious, with lighting along the wall that seemed to be powered by something more than just electricity, their glow a soft gold that seemed to sparkle.

The place offered a sense of awe and security, but I still couldn't help but worry that none of this was real.

I couldn't possibly be safe. I wanted to ask Basir what had happened to Ivan, but I was scared of the answer. If he was dead, I would feel nothing. But if he was alive, which I assumed he was based on Basir's earlier comment about him, then I couldn't truly live without fear. Ivan had wanted me dead, and the man was never refused.

"Sit. Let me get you some food," Basir said as we made our way into a massive dining hall. It was mostly empty, with the exception of a few small groups that looked our way, but the smell of food in the air was heavenly. I nodded as I took the seat he offered, wrapping my arms around myself and watching as he moved across the space with an ease and confidence I envied.

"Three-one-four. You're up."

My eyes widened as I snapped my head to the left, watching as Ravina of all people walked toward me, her words softened by the slight smile on her face.

"Ravina?" I sat up straighter. "You're here—you made it out!" I hadn't realized how much that mattered to me as my eyes stung. Ravina and I may not have been friends, but I wouldn't forget the way she kept showing up those last couple days in the compound.

As she sat down across from me, I immediately noticed a difference in her. There was a glow to her skin, and her dark hair hung in a silky wave to her waist. She was dressed similarly to myself but in all black, the coat wrapped around her shoulders like a shield against the world.

"Of course I did," she scoffed. "The minute they blew those walls in, I was running. That asshole Colyn tried to stop me, but I managed to get away. When Zev saw me make it through the wall and over the rubble, he offered me a spot on his helicopter. Woke up here."

"Zev?" I asked curiously, noticing the way she'd hesitated over his name before continuing on.

"Yeah, he's some captain." She waved the thought of him away with her hand, but her ears turned pink. He was someone important to her—or was *becoming* someone important to her. "He's shown me around the past few days. I'd always heard the Ironsun Pack territory was beautiful, but this place is something else."

"I've only seen a little, but it does seem unreal," I agreed. "I'm glad you made it out, though. I feel bad for the ones who didn't." So much so that I felt like I couldn't breathe for a minute. Who'd been left behind? Had any of the children made it out?

Ravina's face filled with a flash of regret. "Only

some of us escaped...but maybe with the information we've given them, they'll be able to save others." It was a very optimistic tone for her, but I appreciated it. I wanted that to be the case.

The silence between us grew as I considered the implications of everything that had happened. Of how unlucky others had been.

"I'm surprised the three of them even let you out of their sight," Ravina commented, trying to break the somber mood. "They've been guarding you religiously. The Eight would be impressed."

"Really?" I asked. "I've only seen Basir so far. He's getting me food."

Before she could respond, her spine straightened as she looked toward the door. I was confused for only a moment before a large man came striding in, his icy blue gaze darting around the room...before landing on Ravina.

"Shit," she murmured, offering me an eye roll. "While I would love to chat more, three-one-four, I have a feeling Zev is about to interrupt us."

Zev was huge, and as he made his way toward us, he seemed to only get larger—like the size of Ravik. His white-blonde hair was messy, and he looked rumpled, as if he'd just rolled out of bed. Ravina stood in a rush, looking flustered.

"You left bed." His words were filled with concern, and my brows went straight up.

"Hey." Ravina scowled at me, blushing bright pink. "It's not what you think. He just won't let me stay anywhere else. Don't judge."

The unexpected vulnerability that tinged her voice had me immediately assuring her. "I wasn't," I promised. "I was just surprised by how upset he seemed."

"Of course I'm upset," Zev said before offering me a nod in greeting. "Gracie, it's nice to finally meet you. Now come on, baby. Back to the room."

Wait...how did he know my name? Ravina sighed and shook her head at the man, though she wasn't really bothered by his statement as she took his offered hand. Before the two of them left, she offered me a small nod.

"Glad you're awake and safe, three-fourteen. I'm sure I'll see you soon."

And then they were gone.

Three-fourteen. *Not three-one-four.* The change was small, almost nothing, but it caught at me anyway. Softer. Kinder.

Warmth filled my chest as I stared at their retreating forms. Ravina was safe and seemingly happy. But the warmth faded as I thought about others who deserved the same. Others who'd been left behind. The guilt of being one of the few who'd escaped started to grow and feel more oppressive. I tightened my hands on my lap, staring at the wood table in front of me.

All of those children, left to Ivan and his cruel punishments. They were surely suffering because of what happened that night. Frustrated tears welled in my eyes because there was nothing I could do about it. It was like losing Owen all over again, that sense of helplessness.

Maybe I could talk to Ravik or Thornar about it...or Basir. Where was he? I thought he'd have been back by now. My head moved up as I realized the man was nowhere in sight.

In fact, I was completely alone. I was surrounded by strangers, completely alone. My throat started to tighten and I sank further into my chair, feeling the intense need to disappear. Especially when I noticed others looking my way, as if my distress was obvious. It probably was.

"Lil flame, I don't like that look on your face."

Relief cascaded through me. Thornar was right behind me, staring down at me in concern. His large, rough hand smoothed up my throat in a hold that made me melt as his warm brown and golden gaze ran over my expression. His levity was gone, replaced with concern over me. I inhaled his intoxicating scent, and I had to force myself to stay in my seat, to not stand and throw myself into his arms.

"What's wrong?" he asked seriously, his gaze

darting up and looking around the room. "And where's Basir?"

"He went to get me food," I explained softly.

Thornar leaned down and brushed his nose against mine, sending a shiver across my skin. My eyes closed as I imagined him leaning down closer and brushing his lips against my cheek—or even my lips. My hand smoothed up his arm and onto his large hand at my throat. I would have happily stayed like that forever, and my wolf was thrilled—jumping around playfully with shadows, as if interacting with Thornar's wolf.

My anxiety faded into nothing in his presence. Warmth. Safety. Affection. Thornar evoked that and so much more.

"Where were you?" Thornar asked suddenly. His voice held a note I'd never heard before—a dominance and authority that had me feeling almost...defensive for Basir.

"What happened?" Basir asked, concerned and confused, as he set a plate in front of me. My stomach tightened at the sight, my mouth practically watering.

"He was getting me food," I reminded Thornar.

"She shouldn't be alone," Thornar told Basir before sitting next to me.

Basir frowned before tapping my plate. "Eat up, glow. I'm sorry I took so long. One of the captains approached me about a behavioral issue, so I had to direct him down the chain."

"Ah." Thornar sighed and shook his head. "We have a chain of command for a reason. Eat up, Gracie." The second reminder finally spurred me into action.

"What happened?" Basir asked again, directing the question to me. After four or so bites, I finally found it in me to pause and give them the best answer I could manage.

"I was thinking about all of the kids left behind with Ivan. Everyone, really. I can only imagine what he's doing to punish them. I was thinking how lucky I am that you three decided to help some of us, even if it was just for intel on your end."

Thornar broke into a chuckle. "Is that what Basir told you? That it was for intel?"

"I mean, not exactly..."

"We came to get you, lil flame. The intel is just a bonus."

Basir stayed silent, but Thornar's declaration brought a blush to my cheeks as his eyes sparkled with warmth. "Oh. I didn't know that...but why?"

Thornar's expression morphed into something more serious as he tilted my chin up. After a long moment, he spoke in a gentle tone that felt reserved for me. "A conversation to have with all of us present. But trust me, Gracie, that mission had little to do with intel and everything to do with you."

Those words meant the world to me. I didn't know how Basir felt about the statement, though, because Thornar began asking him about the behavioral issue he'd had to handle with his soldiers. Still, for the moment, my heart felt less heavy. The anxiety weighing on my chest had eased, and I allowed myself to eat in peace, enjoying the comfort of these two perfect men.

I didn't know why they'd wanted to save me, but I was thankful for it.

Even if I had nothing else—even if they didn't return my affection—the fact that they'd thought I was worth saving would have to be enough. I couldn't let my stronger emotions cloud the gratitude I should feel...even if every moment around them made my head spin and heart beat in a way I'd never experienced before.

"When you're done eating, I want to give you a tour of this place," Thornar said as I put down my fork, nodding eagerly. I wanted to ask them where Ravik was, but I wasn't brave enough. I longed for him to show up soon. The last memory I had of him was his arms wrapped around me as he carried me out of the compound...

I wanted to know and see that he was okay.

Once I was finished eating, the three of us stood and made our way toward the door of the dining hall. The fresh air felt good against my skin as Thornar wrapped his massive arm around my shoulder, Basir walking beside us.

"Thornar!" a feminine voice called. My wolf stood defensively, letting out a low rumble. Moving further into Thornar, it only took a moment to see who had called his name—a gorgeous woman standing at the bottom of the next set of stairs.

Who was that? And more importantly, who was she to Thornar?

CHAPTER 16
GRACIE

"ELOWEN, aren't you supposed to be teaching right now?"

I hated the warmth in Thornar's voice, but I stuck close to his side as we walked down the steps. I didn't like the way this woman looked at him *or* spoke to him. Basir's hand grazed my back, snapping me out of it.

What was wrong with me? I had no claim on these men. We may have had some forged connection through the aftershocks of the ritual, but for me to assume that they would want me to be so territorial...

I stopped hard on the stairs, and Basir offered me a questioning look. Thornar's expression was far more understanding, though, as he turned toward me and offered a hand, his smile softer than before.

"You don't have to stop scenting me, Gracie, but I promise you have nothing to worry about."

Had I been scenting him? How did he know what I was feeling? I was learning that Thornar had an uncanny ability to directly pinpoint what I needed to hear.

Without a word, I glued myself back to his side, embarrassed for my extreme possessiveness...though not enough to stop. If Thornar was bothered by it, he didn't act like it. He only pulled me tighter against him, infusing comfort into my very bones.

Elowen was painfully gorgeous.

I never felt beautiful, but it didn't take much for me to recognize when others were. She was only about three inches taller than I was, but she held herself with an air of authority that was beyond intimidating.

Her defined, voluminous curls created a natural halo around her angular face, and her rich almond-toned complexion glowed warmly beneath her dark outfit. A high-neck black blouse with sheer sleeves wrapped around her torso and paired perfectly with a black wool skirt that tightened at her tiny waist.

What caught my attention the most, though, was the onyx stone on her nose. I couldn't remember the last time I'd seen a piercing of any kind. That type of self-expression wasn't allowed in the Cold Moon Pack. The idea of it was laughable.

She observed us with curious and fixed interest,

but I didn't see any anger or betrayal at the way Thornar or Basir were interacting with me. It made me feel slightly better, ruling out her potential as someone having a more *complicated* relationship with either of them...but I still was silent as we reached the bottom of the stairs and approached her.

"Am I supposed to be *teaching*?" Elowen demanded, placing her hands on her hips. "Of course I'm supposed to be teaching!" Then she waved a hand toward me in an exasperated and dramatic sweep. "But I can't possibly work knowing my potential new best friend is just across town! You may be my brother, but the three of you have no right to hog her. We *all* want to meet her."

"Brother?" I asked, eyes wide with hope. What Elowen was saying hit me like warmth through frost —not just that Thornar was her *brother*, but that she wanted to be my best friend. I wasn't sure I had ever called anyone a best friend, even my own brother.

"Yes, Thornar's my brother." Her brown eyes sparkled with humor. "Terrible, isn't it?"

"My little flame here would never side with you," Thornar growled, my cheeks flaming as he pulled me completely flush with him again. Basir leaned against the wall, watching all of this with a faint echo of amusement that I found fascinating to watch play across his face.

"*She* has a name." Elowen rolled her eyes before looking at me. "What's your name?"

"Gracie." I cracked a smile. Elowen's outgoing vigor instantly put me at ease, her open and transparent way of talking allowing me to relax into our conversation.

"*Gracie*, it is wonderful to meet you." She smiled brightly. "I hope you don't mind me crashing the tour. I had a feeling these two were about to drag you around the city, and *look*, I was right!" She shot Thornar a pointed look. "And I cancelled my classes, so don't worry about that. I'm not in jeopardy of losing my job, I promise."

"I'm your older brother. I worry about all types of shit." He shrugged in amusement before looking down at me to gauge how I was feeling. "But sure, join us."

Wiggling out of Thornar's grasp, I straightened my shoulders and stood next to Elowen. I didn't have a full grasp on this positive socialization thing outside of a few people in the compound, but I knew I needed to step out of the protective warmth of Thornar eventually. I really didn't want to, but I wanted to make a good impression.

"The elevator is this way!" she chimed.

"You're a teacher?" I asked as we turned down a hallway to the left.

"Yes! Solkaran University—one of the most prestigious universities in all of Thornfell—is right here in our very own capital city. I'm a doctoral student there, so I also teach undergraduates in my 'spare time'."

"Wow," I whispered, trying not to feel a stab of insecurity about my lack of education. "What do you study?"

"Ethical Structures of Empire." Elowen's voice was filled with pride. "I focus mainly on the morality and ethical struggles we find in pack structures. More so, how hostile takeovers and dominance fights can affect the general population."

"A bit intense, isn't it?" Thornar asked from behind us as we reached a glass elevator.

Before the raids, I had been in an elevator once while visiting a larger city within our territory, but it was nothing like this. You could see in every direction through the glass, and the gold accents shimmered like it was made of magic rather than mechanics.

"Intense...but also really interesting," I admitted. "My territory was taken over by Ivan Rivers around a decade ago, so I saw that firsthand."

Elowen's expression turned thoughtful. "I've heard the stories about the Cold Moon Pack. It reminds me of where we came from, although far worse."

Thornar hummed in agreement as we began to descend, the sensation of dropping making me feel unsteady. Basir, somehow knowing this was the case, put a hand against my lower back to stabilize me.

"What happened to your pack?" I asked once I was sure I wouldn't be sick.

"A story for another day," Elowen said, a hint of sadness in her gaze. "I would love to sit down and tell you, though, if Thornar is comfortable with it."

My gaze moved up to him, his eyes warming in pleasure at my attention—as if it made him happy that I looked to him for his feelings about the situation.

"Gracie can ask any question she wants. I'll always answer."

The surety of this man was...*perfection*.

Elowen made an amused noise as the elevator door opened with a ping. "You are already in *so* deep."

What did that mean? Basir made a sound that seemed to be agreement as the four of us stepped out onto the ground floor of the building.

My questions were forgotten pretty quickly, though, as I found myself captivated by the Ironsun Pack's capital city.

As we walked through the open-air atrium, bustling with people dressed in cold-weather clothes and bright smiles on their faces, I tried to catch each and every detail. The bridges between the floors above us were littered with people going about their day, and the mix of steel and stone gave a regal yet modern feel to the building.

It was truly a castle, and I could see that reflected

even in the smallest details—like the stone floor, each section imprinted with the pack's crest.

"I wish it was warmer. It's gorgeous here during the summer months," Elowen promised as we walked through an archway and onto the city streets.

"This *is* gorgeous," I said under my breath as the cool mountain air brushed over me in an exhilarating wave. Even the streets were meticulously clean, iron streetlamps standing proudly with banners all the way down the central street.

Uniformed soldiers moved in groups out of a building to my left, and small children wearing red blazers waved to them excitedly as they walked in a line led by a woman around my age. Scholars buried in books strode into the castle-like building we'd come out of, and cream and red-robed women laughed openly in their conversation.

Life radiated from this city, and the sun itself seemed to shine down on every one of its citizens.

"Come on, glow." Basir's voice was soft and filled with understanding of my awe as he led me forward, Thornar and Elowen having a lively conversation I'd missed the start of.

"She needs to see the temple anyway! It just so happens that Solenne is there." Elowen waved her brother off as Thornar crossed his arms, an amused smile playing at his lips. "Gracie, you want to meet Ravik's sister, right?"

"Yes," I immediately confirmed, because if we were meeting Ravik's sister, maybe Ravik would be nearby. Although, I had to admit that all of the family dynamics I was being introduced to made me feel the void in my own life.

Is this what life would have been like for me and Owen if Ivan had never raided our farm? Would we have been friends like we'd been as kids? It was almost impossible to imagine.

"Plus, Solenne is *big* into giving blessings," Elowen said. "Never a bad thing, right? Always a good idea to keep The Eight watching out for you."

That nearly brought me to a stop. *The Eight* —Nyxarra.

I stared off into the distance as we continued walking, my thoughts racing. The ritual. Something had happened at the end. My memory was still fuzzy, but now that I'd been awake for a few hours, pieces were beginning to click together. Nyxarra had sobbed, begged me to understand that her will wasn't my death. There had been another force, something darker that had threatened to consume her.

The rescue had interrupted the ritual, but something had changed beyond that. A connection had snapped into place between the four of us. Not just instinct. Not just magic. Something *other*. I didn't have the words yet, but I felt the weight of it.

I needed to talk to the three of them about what had happened. Figure out what *this* truly was.

"Isn't it beautiful?"

Elowen's words drew me from my thoughts, making me realize I'd been trapped in them for some time. So much so that I could feel both Thornar and Basir staring at me in concern. My eyes widened as I took in the building we approached, a bridge over a rushing river of icy water separating us from it.

"The Solspire," she continued in explanation, "the largest temple to Vorrakar in Thornfell."

I understood where it got its name. The cone-shaped temple was ten stories tall with a massive glass sun-like ornament decorating the top. The walls, made of glass and iron, reflected the blue skies above, and the ornate red and gold flags whipping in the wind lined the bridge and staircase up toward the front archway.

Considering everything I'd been through, a temple was the last place I wanted to be, but even I could admit that it was a sight to see. My wolf watched it warily but didn't protest as we began to make our way across the bridge.

"Do you worship all of The Eight or just Vorrakar?" I asked the three of them.

"Oh, all of them, but he's for sure the most popular," Elowen answered.

"There's no penalty for not worshipping, though,"

Basir said. When I met his gaze, I could see that he understood my concern. I didn't know *how* he understood it, or if I was just obvious in my trepidation, but I appreciated the assurance.

As we stepped off the bridge, I looked forward to the temple and drew to a stop. My gaze went all the way up to the top and then to the archway, where incense holders drifted in the wind. Something about the vision made my stomach tighten uncomfortably, and I dug my nails into my palms.

"Everything okay, glow?" Basir's voice was rough but comforting...and then he *touched* me.

Rage-filled screams erupted in my head, ripping a cry from my throat as my knees gave out beneath me. The scent of burning flesh slammed into my senses, suffocating and cruel.

My fingers clutched at my skull, wet, slick blood dripping between them and seeping through my hair. Stone bit into my skin as I fell, my body seizing.

The screams only grew louder, a violent crescendo that drowned out the world. My vision went black. I couldn't see. Couldn't feel anything past the pain.

Then it stopped. The cacophony dimmed to a lull as warm muscles held me securely, my body trembling in relief.

"Open your eyes, *lux mea*."

Ravik. My eyes snapped open, but the first person I saw wasn't him. It was Basir.

The man's face was twisted in agony as he looked down at his hand, still outstretched from when he had touched me. *No.* I didn't want him blaming himself for what had just happened to me. It hadn't been his fault. I wanted to get up, to tell him—

"Gracie, look at me."

My eyes moved up to Ravik's intense gaze, ravaged with worry as he held me possessively and molded my body to his. The scent of steel and fresh linen slowed my heartbeat, and let out a shaky breath, unsure of what to say to him or how to explain.

When I looked to Basir for help, he was gone.

CHAPTER 17
RAVIK

GRACIE'S CRUMPLED expression held every ounce of my focused attention as I waited for color to fuse back into her cheeks. Adrenaline surged through my veins, and my heart beat wildly as I tightened my grip on her, not truly hearing anything around me outside of her slowing breaths. I would never forget the scene I'd just walked in on.

I'd been frustrated by my responsibilities every day since Gracie came home with us. But something about today made it worse. Knowing she'd eventually wake was one thing, but realizing she had woken up and was already moving through our city without me?

I trusted Thornar and Basir with my life—and now hers—but nothing would replace having her by my side, where I could ensure her safety myself.

After leaving a heated meeting with my captains about the Cold Moon Pack's recent movement, I'd tracked Gracie across the city, following her vanilla and cinnamon scent—only to find her seizing on the ground. Smoke had surrounded her, black but sparkling under the sun, and all I'd been able to do was pick her up as Thornar shouted for his sister to run into the temple to find help.

When Gracie's seizures had stopped and her eyes opened, I felt relief—and fear. How could we predict something like that? What if one of us hadn't been around to help? Although, if the look on Basir's face told me anything, he blamed himself for what had happened, believing his touch had hurt her.

"I don't understand what happened," I said harshly. Thornar snapped his gaze back around, looking in the same direction as Gracie. I didn't try to look for Basir.

When the bastard wanted to disappear, it was impossible to find him—or to see him coming. It was one of the many things that made him the best choice for Enforcer.

"I felt strange as we got close to the temple, but then when Basir touched me, it seemed to instigate something. The screams and pain were so horrible, and I felt like there was blood everywhere..." She didn't quite finish the sentence, seemingly trapped and reliving the moment once again.

"Come on, let's get you inside," Thornar suggested as I strode into the Solspire with Gracie in my arms.

It was almost impossible not to be distracted by how beautiful she looked today, like there was a flame flickering just beneath her skin. Those gold eyes were filled with caution, but also a life that had been dimmed at the trade conference. The only thing that kept me focused on the task at hand and not absorbed by her presence was the knowledge that the sooner we got her inside, the sooner someone could assure me that she was okay.

Bringing her inside also satisfied my wolf, who was raging at the fact that so many people were looking at Gracie. It was my fault—it wasn't every day that your future Alpha carried a collapsed woman through the street—but this wasn't just any woman. This was *lux mea*.

"Basir will be back, little flame." Thornar was staring at Gracie with concern, her gaze fixed over my shoulder. She gave a nod, but I could tell she didn't believe him—not completely.

"What happened?" My sister rushed into the room, the door to her private shrine thrown open in her haste. Solenne spent most of her days buried in work here at the temple, but her reasons were only partially related to duty. It was the *only* place that she and her mate could be together all day without question.

The priestesses and priests of the Solspire were not supposed to take mates. Their lives were supposed to be dedicated to worshipping Vorrakar. The universe didn't seem to agree, though, and had placed Solenne and Isara in the same profession so they could spend their days together without judgment.

"She passed out on the stairs, started to have seizures," I answered as Solenne ushered us inside her shrine. Thornar shut the door behind us, Elowen staying on the other side. The shrine was barely large enough for two people, let alone five or six.

"But why? What happened?" my sister demanded. Solenne may have been my younger sister, but she'd always acted with a wisdom far beyond her years. And she was aware of who Gracie was to me—to *us*.

If I had it my way, everyone in our territory would know that as well.

The city was large, but news traveled fast. The Cold Moon raid and its fallout had spread quickly, and everyone wanted to know why we'd gone. My commanders—and even my father—might not like the truth, but it was simple: Gracie.

"Breathe, Sol. Let's work backward and first see how she's doing," Isara said, motioning for Gracie's hand. *Lux mea* offered it hesitantly, and I could see how fast her pulse was moving in her neck. Her body was clearly still reeling from what had happened.

"Of course." Solenne offered Gracie a small smile.

"I wish we were meeting in better circumstances, Gracie. I'm Ravik's sister, Solenne, and this is Isara."

Gracie nodded, but I could tell she felt overwhelmed. Tipping her head up with my fingers beneath her chin, I saw the fear there—the confusion.

"How do you feel?" I asked, trying to distract her from the two women checking her vitals. I tried to tone down the forceful and demanding nature of my questions, feeling an aggressive, almost unbearable need to check over every inch of her myself.

"I don't know. After the ritual, something similar happened, but this came out of nowhere. I'm scared, Ravik."

Those words fractured my chest. I leaned down and pressed my forehead to hers, unable to stop the urge to get closer to her. "I vow to you, we will figure this out."

I didn't understand the nature of our bond, whether it was a mate bond or something more, but I did know that I was connected to Gracie more deeply than I'd ever been to anyone.

I could feel her fear.

I could sense her reaching for grounding.

Gracie was accepting my protection, but she needed more—she needed answers.

"I don't see any external injuries, and her vitals seem okay," Isara said.

"So why?" Solenne demanded, looking from me to

Gracie. "You said something about a ritual and that it had happened before..."

"When we rescued Gracie, she was being sacrificed in a ritual to Nyxarra," Thornar said.

"When we took her from the altar, something happened—it created a connection between the four of us," I finished.

Gracie tensed in my arms. Was she surprised I spoke openly about the connection, or about what my statement meant? Surely she recognized this connection as a mating bond. Dread tightened in my chest as I looked down at her, but her eyes were locked on my sister and Isara.

Gracie was mine—but did she want to be? I hadn't even questioned it until now.

No. I had to believe that she did. There was no way she reacted to me as she did—melting into my touch —without knowing something existed between us.

"Like a mating bond?" Isara asked, surprised.

"And something more," Thornar confirmed.

"More?" my sister echoed. "The Eight offer mating bonds as a guiding suggestion, not a forceful action— it's formed through the fulfillment of physical and emotional ties. What you're suggesting is...something else. I don't have a word for it."

Of course, Solenne was right. Normally, mate bonds were formed by mating in the traditional, physical sense, and through a vow ceremony witnessed by loved ones. It was only in the oldest texts—ancient tomes in our library—that other types of bonds were mentioned: *mates tethered to one another by fate.*

Was that what we had been gifted?

A possessive wave of relief washed over me as I looked down at Gracie, her cheeks flushed pink and her eyes filled with confusion. Not ideal, but it was better than the fearful look that had been there moments ago.

Thornar was surprisingly quiet as he smoothed a hand over Gracie's shoulder, then gently ran his fingers through the ends of her braided hair. I could guess what he was thinking, and I had no doubt he'd make his feelings clear very soon. He wasn't one to hold back.

"That wasn't the only thing that happened." Gracie's voice was soft as she straightened, pulling on a strength that sent pride surging through me. There was no doubt Gracie was strong, but I knew it would take time for her to fully recognize it.

We would surround her with shields until she was ready to charge into battle herself.

"When I was laying on the altar, I had a vision," she said, her gaze going distant. "It was the goddess Nyxarra, but she was sobbing...begging. She screamed that this ritual wasn't her will. I don't know why, and maybe I'm misinterpreting, but she felt...trapped? As if she were being held captive or someone was forcing her hand. I don't know how that would even be possible, but I can still hear her cries."

Gracie's words held both truth and a shocking amount of new information. I watched her in surprise as Solenne and Isara fell silent.

"That...that is quite the vision," Isara finally said, frowning as she looked at my sister. "We should do a ritual blessing—but more like an analysis. I think it'll give us better answers."

"Are you okay with that?" I asked Gracie, and she nodded immediately.

I looked to Thornar, who seemed as conflicted as I felt. If simply walking into a temple had triggered that reaction, what would an analysis do?

For the next ten minutes, my sister and her mate created a ritual circle around us. They'd asked Thornar and me to move, but the panic that overtook Gracie's face had us sitting on either side of her instead. My hand wrapped around her waist while Thornar kept her distracted with light, relaxed conversation. The bastard was far better at that than I was.

After what Gracie had undergone, rituals of any kind—any ceremony—understandably terrified her.

When Isara and Solenne began to speak soft words around us, our conversation stopped immediately. Gracie froze. My attention locked on her face, searching for any sign of pain, ready to stop the ritual the moment she showed distress. But instead, she just looked nervous.

When my sister approached, stepping into the circle, Gracie relaxed. "Your hands," my sister said gently, motioning for Gracie to take hers. The air sparked once their fingers touched, the circle on the floor lighting up with a bright glow.

There was a magic that existed beyond shifting and our connection to The Eight—something older. Primordial. We didn't have a name for it, but you could feel it pulsing through our territory, through the entire country. Some people could tap into it, and my sister was one of them.

White smoke began to roll over Gracie's fingers and climb up her arms. If it scared *lux mea*, she didn't show it. She just watched Solenne's face with quiet curiosity.

After three painstakingly long minutes, Solenne stepped back and took a deep breath. The silence that followed was heavy as she and Isara began to clean up without saying anything.

Almost immediately, I gave in to the urge to run my hand up Gracie's back and onto her neck, massaging the skin there lightly. When she tensed, I immediately stilled in confusion, meeting her wide-eyed gaze.

"What's wrong?"

"I...nothing," she murmured, breaking eye contact

in a way that had a low rumble forming in my throat. I may have been an Alpha, but the last thing I wanted was for my mate to feel like she had to look away from me.

Thornar let out a low rumble, not satisfied with her answer either. "You've got to tell us when something bothers you, Gracie. Otherwise we won't know to stop."

Gracie blinked at his blunt honesty, and after a long moment she nodded in understanding before looking back at me. "I just wasn't expecting your touch to be soft there. Ivan usually held me really hard on the back of my neck, and I was surprised that your touch felt different."

Her admission made my wolf growl deep in my chest, restrained but vicious. A flash of Ivan's throat being torn out played through my mind. The bastard had escaped my wrath thus far, but every word Gracie said about him fueled the torture I planned to deliver.

"The minute you don't want me to, just tell me," I said, voice low and serious.

She nodded immediately, then melted between the two of us. I had so much to learn about Gracie, and the last fucking thing I ever wanted was to scare her. Or worse, hurt her.

I had never walked on eggshells or lived cautiously. It wasn't in my nature. But I found myself willing to do that and so much more just to ensure she was comfortable and happy.

"We need to talk," Solenne said, drawing our attention back. Isara was sitting across the room, flipping through a large text with rapt attention, searching for something.

"Never a good thing to say," Thornar muttered. "It might be better to tell us what's going on."

"The four of you are tethered," Solenne confirmed, and Gracie nodded—her wordless agreement matching what we'd all felt.

"But you aren't just tethered as mates. Your bond contains a god scar."

"A god scar?" I had never heard the term.

"It's a mark on your mating bond from one of The Eight—Nyxarra, specifically. It marks you as a champion of theirs. A chosen one," Isara explained, carrying her book toward us and setting it on the table. "This book has a lot of information on the mythology behind it, but..."

"But what?" Thornar asked, reading the shift in her tone.

Solenne exhaled, finishing her mate's thought. "Honestly? We've never actually heard of or met anyone who's been a Vessel of The Eight. It makes sense, considering what you've told us, Gracie. But it's still shocking."

Isara's expression was somber. "I wouldn't tell

others about it—at least not until you figure out *why* Nyxarra marked you."

Gracie's voice was quiet but certain. "I think her vision made it clear. I think she needs help. And I am—we are—supposed to help her."

Thornar's voice was low. "But who has the power to imprison a god?"

That was a damn good question.

CHAPTER 18
GRACIE

THE SOFT, distant sound of a television brought my heavy eyes to open—the world around me bathed in heat, comfort, and confusion. The first two probably had to do with the proximity of a very warm, masculine chest underneath my cheek. Something I didn't allow myself to process just yet, because I knew my face would turn bright red.

Thornar's deep, rhythmic breathing and solid heartbeat removed any trepidation as I tried to piece together the past few hours. Or maybe it had been longer than that.

Following the revelation in the Solspire, both Ravik and Thornar had brought me back to their home before all but barricading the doors. Of course, it hadn't been that extreme, and I was pretty sure I could leave at any moment—but why would I want to?

Especially when we'd spent most of the afternoon and evening just...*being.*

After everything I'd been through, it was impossible to ignore the simplicity and pleasure of existing without pain—without fear. But that was what they provided: a structure I felt like I could finally breathe into.

After a few hours of Thornar's amusing comments and Ravik's intense yet comforting presence, my cheeks had even hurt from smiling. We'd played several board games and even watched a few shows, one of which Thornar found particularly amusing. And when Ravik made a dinner of steak and soft, seasoned potatoes, I hadn't hesitated to eat second servings, because even the little I knew from the men made me aware that was what they would want.

But the evening had been missing an essential element: *Basir.*

He'd never come back, and while we hadn't spoken about Solenne or Isara's revelation or what had brought us to them in the first place, I had a feeling they were concerned about Basir's absence as well. It had been less than a day, but it was obvious how close the three men were. Essentially brothers. The guilt of playing a part in Basir's absence weighed heavily on me, especially since he still hadn't returned by the time I'd fallen asleep on the couch.

The last thing I wanted was for Basir to feel like he couldn't be in his own home.

Trying to shake myself from that thought, I slowly shifted away from Thornar and his large chest. I looked down at the gorgeous man, a wash of embarrassment filling my cheeks.

I was in bed...with Thornar. His massive frame was spread out, an arm behind his head and his chest rising in slow, even breaths. It was unfair how beautiful he was, and I found myself staring, almost in awe, before I forced myself from bed.

I had no idea how we'd gotten from the couch into the bedroom, but if he woke up, I'd have no idea what to say to him. I was glad, in a way, that it was just him. I didn't know where Ravik was, but the idea of both of them in bed with me was almost too much to bear.

I quickly made my way into the closet, grabbing a pile of clothes and taking them into the bathroom attached to the suite. I breathed out a small sigh as I closed the door and leaned my body against the surface. What in The Eight was I doing?

Turning toward the large vanity mirror, I wrapped my arms around my waist, noticing that I looked... different. My hair hung loose around my shoulders, and I was wrapped in an oversized shirt that Ravik had given me. It felt surreal to see myself standing in a bathroom so opulent and gorgeous, while being so relaxed and comfortable.

This wasn't the life I'd ever thought I'd live.

I had to make sure not to take this for granted. I had no idea what the future would hold. This could be a temporary reprieve, so I would enjoy it as much as possible.

Thankfully, Ravik had shown me how to turn on the shower yesterday. The many dials and knobs had confused me at first, much to my embarrassment, but this morning I was able to take a quick shower. There was no way I'd have been able to fall back asleep—not with so much on my mind. The clock on the vanity read nearly six in the morning, but I felt energized, my body not used to the amount of sleep—nor the quality —I'd just been given.

Within fifteen minutes, I was ready for the day, dressed in an oversized green sweater with velvet bows on the shoulders. The rest of my clothes were simple—black pants and black boots—but the sweater entertained me as I fixed my hair with a similar ribbon to keep it out of my face.

When I stepped out of the bathroom, I was relieved to see Thornar still sleeping. I would have felt guilty for waking him, especially after our long and eventful day yesterday.

Leaving the bedroom and walking down the corridor toward the foyer, I thought about everyone I'd met. Elowen had been amazing, and though I hadn't been able to talk to her after the ritual in the temple, I knew I'd probably see her soon. She seemed set on being friends, and I hoped I could be a good one. I'd never really had that before.

Then there was Solenne and Isara. Even with everything else going on, I couldn't help but notice how easily they finished each other's sentences—almost magnetic in how naturally they fit together as mates.

Solenne reminded me of a priestess from an old text, her white silk dress flowing around her short curvy frame marked with gold-painted sigils. She carried a calm, familiar warmth, and the way she treated Isara—always checking in before acting—was undeniably sweet, the kind of steadiness anyone would want in a mate.

Isara had a willowy frame wrapped in sapphire fabric, her copper skin marked with silver sigils that echoed Solenne's. Silver rings gleamed on her long fingers and through her onyx braids, catching the light when she moved. There was something protective in the way she watched her mate, her brown eyes softening every time Solenne spoke—like a wolf content to guard what mattered most.

I felt lucky to have witnessed such an authentic display of love.

The front door opened with a whoosh as I slipped out into the early morning air. I hesitated for only a second before letting the door fall shut, hearing the lock click into place.

Well...I supposed it was good that I was dressed and ready for the day.

Standing in the morning stillness with the eerie silence of the Ironsun castle surrounding me, I couldn't help but wonder why I'd left the suite. Was I trying to prove to myself that I could be on my own? Or maybe it was because I'd been fighting the urge to search for Basir for too long. His expression, agonized and guilt-ridden, was still vivid in my mind.

Basir believed his touch had hurt me, but I was more certain than ever that it hadn't been him. After learning about the god scar on our bond, I had a feeling it was simply a reaction—an intense, divine reaction—triggered by our mating connection. It could have happened with any of them; it just happened to be him. And I could feel that it had awakened something in him too—something that was keeping him away.

Or maybe it was bigger than that. Maybe Basir understood exactly what existed between us and didn't want it. Thornar and Ravik hadn't looked surprised when the bond was confirmed, but I couldn't tell if they were happy about it, so it wasn't hard to imagine that Basir might be uncertain, maybe even afraid.

I'd tried so hard to hide my *own* reaction—how

thrilled and relieved I'd been that the bond I felt was real—but I wasn't sure I'd succeeded. That joy had bloomed...until fear crept in.

What if none of them wanted this?

They hadn't asked for the bond, or the tether that came with it. And they certainly hadn't asked to be marked by a god—bound to a goddess who, to me, still represented bloodshed and pain.

Nyxarra was the reason so many had died in the Cold Moon Pack. Why had she chosen me, now expecting *us* to serve her as champions? Had I been rescued only to fall under a new master, dragging my mates into a future dictated by the gods?

Guilt surged like a wave, hot tears burning behind my eyes. Maybe the reason Basir stayed away and the other two hadn't brought it up last night was the most obvious one:

They might be considering rejecting the bond.

Forcing myself to walk forward, blinking away tears, I made my way down the open-air hallway in search of something to occupy my mind. I knew the only thing that would fix this was asking them, but I realized pretty quickly I had no idea where to look.

After thirty minutes of wandering the first two floors, I made my way to the nearest living space I could find—a floor down and opposite the dining room from yesterday. There was almost no one around except soldiers in training gear. I tilted my head, thoughtful. I bet *that* was where Ravik had gone.

The room was cozy, with chairs and soft surfaces arranged around a fireplace, its embers faintly glowing. Morning sunlight poured through a series of glass doors on the far wall, framing a view of the mountains. I was drawn to the balcony, stepping outside and catching my breath—not just from the altitude but from the view.

My fingers tightened on the railing as I looked down, then back up, a wave of nausea rising in my throat. Heights made my skin crawl, and standing here only proved it.

"You eventually get accustomed to it."

A jolt of adrenaline surged through me as I tensed, snapping my head to the side. A woman stood several feet away, in almost the same position as me. Her gaze was fixed on me with polite interest, then she offered a small smile.

"I'm sorry, I didn't mean to interrupt," I said quickly. Humor sparked in her navy-blue eyes, softening her sharp, elegant features.

"You didn't interrupt—I didn't announce myself either," she said with a light laugh, leaning forward to look out over the railing. The wind teased her hair, which was piled elegantly on top of her head. I couldn't quite gauge her age—perhaps mid-fifties— but she radiated a maternal warmth that blended with a wild strength just under the surface, fierce and undeniable. I couldn't tell which part of her was truer, or how she carried both so effortlessly.

Before I could speak, she turned back to me, leaning a hip against the railing and tucking her coat closer around her. "Besides, I've been meaning to talk with you. Hopefully without the overbearing presence of my son. Honestly, I'm shocked he even let you out of his sight."

My eyes widened in surprise, a knot of nervousness tightening in my throat. Her tone was affectionate and teasing, but it didn't make my ability to respond any easier.

"You're Ravik's mom?" I could see the resemblance.

"Yes, but you can just call me Malara. I'm the Luna of the Ironsun Pack—well, until Ravik takes the helm. Then I suspect that will be *your* position."

I blinked once...twice...then exhaled. "I... I'm sorry, I don't even know what to say. I feel torn between wanting to apologize, and at the same time..."

"Breathe, Gracie," she said gently, moving toward a small table and chairs nearby. "Let's sit and talk, *or* answer any questions you have. I promise I won't hold back."

"Do you know *everything*?" I asked, sitting across from her.

"Solenne and Ravik have both updated Deegan

and me about your bond and the interaction with Nyxarra," she confirmed. "Of course, we were also aware of the boys' mission to rescue you. My husband was a bit frustrated at the spontaneity of it, but he worries about everything." Her tone softened affectionately.

"I don't know what to say," I admitted, looking down at my hands. "I haven't had a chance to process it all myself. It's a lot."

"And you shouldn't be rushed," she said reassuringly.

"What's a Luna?" I asked, not sure what the expression meant. Malara's brows lifted in surprise, and I wanted to disappear in my embarrassment. "My formal education ended at eleven when Ivan took over the territory. Before that I lived on the farm...I wasn't exposed to as much as I should have been."

"Eleven is a very young age to experience so much," she murmured, her concern evident. Something seemed to occur to her then, inspiring her to stand. "Walk with me. I want to show you something."

I rose and followed her, keeping pace as she strolled gracefully through the halls. She wasn't a queen, at least not like in the fairy tales my mom would read me as a child, but she moved like one, every step purposeful and composed.

"A Luna is the mate and equal of the Alpha in a pack," she explained. "It's a formal title, but it's not based on dominance—not in the same way Alpha status is. As our society has evolved, those rigid roles have softened. Thornar and Basir, who could each lead as Alphas in their own right, have chosen different paths, showing that our base nature doesn't define us. Instead of feeling combative toward one another, they work beside each other."

"How long have the two of them been in the Ironsun Pack? Or did they grow up here?" I asked. I tried not to linger on the hopeful ache in my chest. If *Luna* meant what I gathered from her explanation, then Malara wasn't just approving the bond. She was affirming it.

"My husband and I took the boys in at twelve and ten, respectively, though they arrived very differently —that's a story they'll want to tell you themselves, no doubt. But we raised them as our own. Even now, they're more like brothers than soldiers. That's one reason my husband has trusted Ravik to lead in his...absence."

Which meant Thornar and Basir didn't have parents. Not here, at least. My chest ached.

I didn't feel comfortable asking about the "absence," so I shared my own story. "I lost my dad the night of the raid and my mom a few years later. It was nice to see that Elowen and Thornar were able to stay together."

She smiled softly. "Elowen is a wildfire. She's been

good for Solenne. My daughter has always been far too cautious." Her expression morphed into one that was more serious. "I'm sorry you lost your parents. I can only imagine the horrors you've lived through, Gracie."

I nodded slowly, taken aback by her depth of emotion and empathy toward someone she barely knew. "I just hope that their choice to rescue me didn't bring danger to your door."

As we reached a long hallway with a purple carved door at the far end, her laughter echoed, full of confidence. "We don't worry about Ivan's forces. There's a reason he hates our pack."

I was starting to understand why. Ivan wielded fear, but here? Here, there was true power—and it was awe-inspiring.

"Here we are." She opened the double doors with an easy turn of a gold handle, and I sucked in a breath.

A library—though the word didn't do it justice.

Towering floor-to-ceiling bookshelves lined the entire length and width of the room, which had three levels. Iron ladders on rails allowed access to the higher shelves, and a stained-glass dome crowned the center of the room, casting a kaleidoscope of morning light onto a plush velvet sitting area below.

"This is beautiful," I whispered as she led me forward, the floor glowing softly in response to our steps. The scent of aged parchment filled the air, accompanied by the faint rustle of pages being turned.

It was serene. Peaceful. And much like being near Malara herself, I felt at ease here. There was a surprising gentleness to her despite the power she wielded.

"This is our family library," she said, gesturing around. "It's open to you, always. You may not have had the opportunity to learn under Ivan's rule, but that won't happen here. No question is forbidden, no piece of knowledge hidden."

"Thank you," I whispered, blinking away the sting in my eyes.

"Enjoy yourself. I'll have breakfast brought here," she added, motioning to the couch. "And if I run into my son, I'll let him know you're perfectly safe."

Would Ravik actually be worried about that?

As she left, a quiet swell of hope rose in my chest. I was deeply grateful, not just for being welcomed so warmly, but for being given this chance. I'd never considered myself unintelligent, but I knew there was a disparity between what I'd been taught and what I had yet to learn.

Maybe I would have a chance to catch up.

I'd never known that something as simple as the possibility of learning could feel so much like healing.

CHAPTER 19
GRACIE

I DIDN'T EXPECT how quickly I'd be absorbed by the vast amount of knowledge around me. The heavy tomes on my lap were filled with fascinating pieces of information that I couldn't even begin to separate or pick through. It must have been hours, the midday sun beaming down from above me, before I forced myself to stand up to return the pile of books I'd collected.

The library was very quiet, my shoes echoing with each step, but it wasn't uncomfortable. In fact, it put my mind at ease. While I would have preferred to see Ravik, Basir, or Thornar, the time alone allowed me to reflect. I felt more grounded than when I'd woken up, and though my chest ached with doubt and vulnerability, I recognized that the only way to resolve this was to *talk* to them.

When I found them, at least.

As I slid the first book back on the shelf and made my way to the second location up a set of stairs to the left side of the room, I passed a table covered with paper, pens, and empty journals. My fingers ran over them as I considered picking one up, even if it just meant writing out my name. It had been forever since I'd held a pen, let alone wrote anything. Communication in written form had been forbidden in the Cold Moon Pack.

The concept of writing almost felt foreign to me. Maybe eventually I'd try again.

When I reached the second story of the library, I easily found where to return the book. Turning, I found myself frozen to the spot, because not even six feet from me, sitting on a chair overlooking the room, was Basir.

His emerald gaze was riveted to me, his body tense as he slowly stood. Shadows cloaked his location in the corner, but as he stepped out of them—not moving any closer—I could see it. I could see the pain on his face as he stared at me, not in surprise, but in caution. As if I would...hurt him?

"Have you been up here for long?" I asked, taking a step closer to him. His fists were clenched so tightly that his veins bulged, and he looked exhausted, as if he hadn't slept.

When he didn't answer, I emboldened myself a bit more, feeling as though I was on the edge of something. This moment was important; I just didn't fully understand why.

"Why didn't you join me, Basir?" Emotion clogged my throat. I'd thought he had been just avoiding me out of guilt...but now he was watching me, but from a distance? I just didn't understand.

Basir's gaze went over my shoulder for a long moment, his fists loosening and tightening again in what appeared to be an act of control. He was stopping himself from doing *something*, and all I wanted to do was to move closer to him.

"I've had meetings about the Cold Moon Pack. I only just got out of them." His words didn't ring false, not completely, and those meetings sounded important, but he also wasn't saying everything. I continued to stare at him for a long moment before his gaze moved back to mine.

"You know," I whispered in realization.

The others had told him everything—about the bond and the god scar. This wasn't just about the guilt from what occurred at the temple. There was a larger fear there.

A sense of loss hit me. I wrapped my arms around myself, trying to stop my lip from dipping, my eyes stinging with heat. I had no right to be sad; he hadn't asked for any of this. But his actions, his distance... They felt like a rejection.

"Yes. They told me—"

I was already turning away, not wanting him to see my tears as I felt my heart fracture just a little bit. I had never expected to find my mate, let alone more than one, but the idea of him rejecting our bond... It was too much.

"Gracie." His voice was warm against my ear as his arm wrapped around my waist, capturing me against him. The man reminded me of a radiator, and as I turned into him, looking up into his expression, I could see his panic. He was worried about my reaction? But that made no sense if he didn't want—

Basir kissed me.

I'd never been kissed before, but the way he slid his hand to cup my jaw while the other tightened on my waist had me melting into it. His lips were warm against my own, and his minty breath intertwined with mine. Heat rushed over my skin, and I couldn't help but tremble, feeling the force and magnitude of our bond rage through the two of us.

Despite the intensity of our kiss, his grip was careful on me, almost reverent. Almost as if he'd never held anyone like this. His kiss was as needy as my own, and it felt like I was drinking from a well of emotion that looped between the two of us endlessly—like undulating waves.

I didn't even realize my hands had slipped into his hair until he ripped his lips away. My breathing was fast, blood roaring through my veins, as he stared down at me with desperate need.

"I shouldn't have—" Basir stopped himself, looking manic and out of sorts as he continued to stare at me, his words finally registering. "No. I won't say that. I don't fucking regret anything about that, glow."

"Please don't regret it."

He moved close again, pressing our foreheads together. "I shouldn't even be touching you, let alone kissing you."

The agony in his voice made my heart break for him. I shook my head, almost angry at him for feeling that way. "I want you to touch...and kiss me. Yesterday wasn't your fault. It could have been any of you that caused that reaction."

I never expected my reassurance to sound so confident, but I could also hear the desperation, the *need* for him to believe me.

Basir shook his head. "Don't say that. Don't say you want me to touch you. It's so much deeper than just yesterday. I shouldn't be anywhere near you."

I hated that. I hated what he was saying.

The words to tell him exactly that were right on the tip of my tongue. I didn't care if it embarrassed me, he needed to know how much I wanted his touch. His kiss. Before I could do that, though, a very familiar voice called out.

"There you are, little flame!" Thornar called as he

made his way up the stairs. Basir's chest released a low rumble as he gripped me tighter, frustrated we were being interrupted.

I turned in Basir's arms, and he kept his arm around me, his forehead pressed to my shoulder. I didn't move too much because I wanted to show him that his touch was good, that I completely and utterly accepted it.

"Basir—should have known you would be here," Ravik called out, seeming amused.

Basir grunted but didn't say anything, keeping me close as Thornar threw himself down in the chair that was now abandoned. "Did you know we were advised to give you space, Gracie?" Thornar shook his head, looking disappointed. "Turns out that was a terrible idea. We lasted exactly three hours, and Basir here didn't last *any* hours."

"Well, yesterday..." I hesitated, not wanting to make him feel bad about needing space.

Ravik, of all people, shook his head, a smile tugging at his lips. "Basir was around yesterday. Don't let him tell you differently."

Basir lifted his head from my shoulder, shooting both men a glare that was frankly terrifying before looking down at me with soft affection. "I made sure you were safe."

I didn't know exactly what that meant, but it was clear that despite not seeing him, he'd been around.

Where did he even get the skillset to move around so silently? It almost seemed *other*.

"Right." I nibbled my lip and then spoke honestly. "We...we probably all need to talk, especially after yesterday."

"What's there to talk about?" Thornar asked. "Didn't I say something about marriage when we first met? And look at that—we're mates. The Eight clearly agree."

His teasing was layered with something deeper, especially with how he was looking at me—a possessive flair filling his warm gaze. It almost was a challenge, as if he wanted me to deny what was so obvious between us...and I found I couldn't. But that didn't remove my other concerns.

"But you didn't ask for any of this."

"Gracie, I think you know exactly how we feel about this situation." Ravik's voice was filled with authority and dominance, making my heart beat wildly. I looked at his serious expression before slipping from Basir's arms and turning toward the three of them.

I could tell he didn't like my distance, but I needed space to think. To formulate how I wanted to tell them what I was worried about.

"A mate bond is one thing, but the god scar and being a vessel? You shouldn't have to deal with that."

"If we're tethered, then it was destined." Basir's

words were quiet, but his gaze was hyper-focused on me, almost predatory—as if he was worried I would walk away. It should have made me feel better, but I couldn't allow myself to truly believe.

"*Lux mea*, why do you think we came for you?"

That question brought me to a stop, because of course I'd asked Basir as much when I first woke. But to have them all surrounding me like this, centered on me—it made me nervous to ask.

"For information. For answers." I was stumbling over my own words, defaulting to the most logical option. Even if their feelings for me played a part in it, to assume that three men would travel across the country to save me was insane.

Thornar shook his head. "We could get that anywhere. We've even had spies within his territory before."

"We came for *you*, glow." Basir's declaration had a delicate and vulnerable belief building inside of my heart. They couldn't be any clearer. These men, before any bond had kicked in, had traveled across the country for me. To save me.

"You really want this? Me?" I hated the words as they came out of my mouth. Why was I asking them to question something that made me so happy?

"That is not in question." Ravik's answer was firm, his gaze filled with a heat and intensity that left me breathless. "You're not going anywhere."

I didn't want to go anywhere.

Thornar flashed me a smile and reached out to offer his hand, my fingers grazing over his. "Want you? I'm obsessed with you, little flame. Probably stared at you for nearly an hour after you fell asleep." My cheeks flamed with color as I finally looked at Basir.

"You're safe now, Gracie."

I believed him. I believed *them*.

"Okay," I whispered, looking down and smiling, trying to shift from the intensity of the emotion wrapped around us. It was almost too much. "But if you do need information, I can try to tell you everything I know. I haven't picked up a pen in years, but I can try to even draw a map of his compound or anything else that would help."

"We may need that," Basir said. "According to our sources, Ivan is less than pleased with our actions."

"But it won't be an issue," Ravik instantly said, relaxing the knot in my chest. "He's always been a thorn in the rest of Thornfell's side. If he calls for war, we won't find a lack of allies."

"I've got a question." Thornar stood, looking around the library's first floor. "How did you manage to find your way in here? I haven't been here for years."

It was such a turn of conversation that it took my brain a minute to catch up. "When I got up this morning—"

"And left bed, something I hated," Thornar pointed

out. His tone light and teasing, so I knew he wasn't actually mad.

"I ran into your mom," I said, looking at Ravik.

He arched his brow. "My mom? And she brought you here?"

"Was she not supposed to?" I asked, feeling a surge of anxiety.

"She just doesn't like anyone," Thornar chuckled. "But that doesn't seem to apply to you at all, Gracie."

My chest ached with happiness and hope. These men wanted me—*me*, not just my information. And maybe...maybe their families did too. The thought felt fragile, almost too much to believe.

They wanted me. *All of me.*

CHAPTER 20
GRACIE

IT WAS A FEW HOURS LATER, while I was eating dinner in the dining hall with the three of them, that I realized —they were skipping meetings just to spend time with me.

"The meeting shouldn't take long. We wouldn't even be going if it wasn't important," Ravik said, his arms folded in front of him in an obvious effort to keep from piling more food onto my already full plate.

"I'm glad you're all eating beforehand, just in case," I said. It probably sounded ridiculous, worrying about whether they were hungry, but I couldn't help it. The thought of them going without—even a little— felt wrong.

Part of me even wanted to cook for them. The instinct was there, but cooking had always been a

211

forced task, and the idea of doing it because I wanted to felt insane. Almost impossible. But maybe not forever. Maybe one day I'd try. Just to see what it felt like to make something and know it was for them.

"Where will you two be?" Basir asked. He sat next to me, and although he wasn't touching me, he was so close I could practically hear his heartbeat. I felt more confident in where I stood with all of them, but Basir was still keeping a physical distance. I just didn't understand why yet.

"That's a surprise." Thornar winked at me, causing my cheeks to flush. "I'm not letting you steal my date ideas."

A date. I'd heard the term before, but that wasn't how things had worked in the Cold Moon Pack. The idea of going on a date with Thornar was...exciting. Terrifying. Too good to be true. It made me feel wanted and special. It caused my heart to—

"Are you sure you don't have to go to the meeting?" I asked in sudden concern. "You're probably supposed to be there too."

"No." Thornar shook his head. "I'll get the notes later. I tend to fall asleep halfway through the meetings as it is."

"Which looks bad," Ravik reminded him.

"So me not going and instead focusing on our date is a benefit to all." His beautiful smile made me relax, seeing that he truly didn't mind missing.

I couldn't deny, though, that Ravik and Basir's departure a few minutes later felt wrong. When the four of us had been together the past few hours, it felt *right*. I really didn't like the separation now.

Luckily, Thornar didn't let me think about it, because the minute I was done eating we were on the move, down the elevator and into the main atrium.

"So do I get to know where we're going?" I teased as he intertwined our fingers together, my heart beating double time at the sweet yet oddly familiar interaction. As if we'd done it every day for years.

"I don't know if I've mentioned it," he murmured, gaze dropping to my lips and pulling to a stop, "but I've got a bit of a sweet tooth." He leaned in, his voice low and warm. "I can't help myself around sweet things."

The way he said it sent color rushing to my cheeks because I was pretty sure he wasn't *just* talking about dessert.

Then we were off again, the whiplash of the moment causing me to almost feel high off of Thornar's energy. It felt exhilarating to just be around him.

"So we're going to get something sweet?" I asked, the brisk night wind rolling over us as we stepped outside. The streetlights were all lit up, casting warm glows over the streets, and I could hear the sounds of celebration in the distance, a sense of joy and excitement filling the air.

"Already have something sweet." Thornar winked at me, his smile bringing one to my own lips. "But yes, it's a place my sister and I visited often when we first came here. Always made us feel better."

"When did you come here?" I asked him, my smile faltering. I didn't want to pry, but I wanted to know more about him. To know *everything* about him.

"When I was around twelve." He looked thoughtful for a minute. "Hard to believe that was fifteen years ago."

I hadn't known how old Thornar—or any of them —was until this moment. It made sense they were older than me, but I hadn't thought to ask.

"Are Ravik and Basir around the same age?"

"Ravik is." Thornar led me across the street, wrapping a protective arm around me before we reached the other sidewalk. "Basir is twenty-five, so two years younger than us."

"I'm twenty-one," I said. Should I have felt weird about being younger than them? It didn't feel like there was a massive age difference between us. I suppose four to six years wasn't really that much.

"And you've probably felt like you've lived ten lifetimes in that," Thornar said in a more solemn tone than usual. "At least, that's what it felt like for me.

When I left our home and made it here, I didn't feel twelve anymore."

"Why did you and your sister have to leave?"

"My father was the Alpha of a pack in Silverpine for decades," he explained quietly, his gaze set on a row of shops ahead of us. "But one of our territorial enemies, a rogue group, challenged him for his position. My father was a proud man, and my mother a warrior. They both died in battle, so my sister and I fled before we could be exiled."

"That's horrible," I whispered, my heart aching. I knew what it felt like to watch your parents die. Thornar's had died in battle, but it didn't take away the sting.

"It left a mark," he admitted before inhaling sharply. "I'd met Ravik when we traveled for a diplomatic trip, and since we were the same age, we became fast friends. I knew that once we crossed into Thornfell, the only place to go was the Ironsun Pack."

We stopped in front of a brightly colored shop, the awning different shades of purple and pink, with a sign on it that read *Sun Sugar*.

Before we moved toward the door, I looked up at him. "If you were meant to be an Alpha, hasn't it been difficult to be in a Beta position?" From what I understood, the urge to be that dominant was almost impossible to ignore.

Thornar chuckled, opening the door into the shop before responding, "No. I saw what the pride of being an Alpha did to my father. I have no intention of following in the same path."

"Thornar! Good to see you!" said an older gentleman standing behind a long, colorful counter.

"Tilo." Thornar's greeting and smile were authentic as the man's warm eyes shifted to me.

"And who is this?"

"Gracie." Thornar's voice was filled with a measure of pride that had never been directed towards me before. I may have been stuck to his side, but I stood straighter at his tone, wanting to make a good impression.

"Wonderful to meet you. Pick anything you want —it's on the house."

"Not necessary, but I know saying that won't stop you," Thornar said. "Go ahead, little flame. Pick what looks good."

Moving to the long row of glass, I was captivated by the rows of confections in every color imaginable. From blocks of fudge dusted with gold to handcrafted truffles set in small wrappers like a pearl in a shell. All of it made my mouth water, but what *really* caught my attention was a series of small pastel sandwich cookies—at least, that was what they looked like. Each side of the cookie was a crispy-soft puff, and between it, a whipped filling.

And there were so many different types!

I was so distracted by them that it took my ears a moment to register the conversation that Tilo was having with Thornar. "...they're sitting out back. I haven't seen them leave, either. I know you told me to keep an eye out on him just in case."

Thornar's demeanor was different from normal, his expression far more serious and calculating. It didn't seem unnatural to him, but it wasn't a version of him I'd seen before, so it made my brow crinkle in confusion.

"Good work, I'll check it out," he assured him before looking over at me, his gaze warm. "Find what you want, little flame?"

"These," I said immediately, looking back down at the pastel cookies.

"A set of macarons coming up." Tilo went to grab a box, and I felt the urge to roll up on my toes in excitement. It was ridiculous, of course, but I couldn't remember the last time I'd even tasted anything with sugar in it.

"I'll be interested to see what you think of these," he mused. "If you end up liking them, we can have them brought home anytime you want."

Liking them was an understatement. Five minutes later, tucked away on the outside patio near an outdoor fireplace eating my new favorite treat, I couldn't express anything but love for them.

"They're like sugar pillows, and every one has a different flavor!" They came in every color and flavor under the sun, from lavender to lemon to even rose.

Thornar chuckled, the sound of it absolutely addicting, his arm wrapped around me as he looked away from the fire and down at me. "I'm glad you love them, and I love seeing how happy they make you. I want to see more of that smile."

Feeling a bit shy at his use of the word *love*, I looked back down at the macarons and admitted, "Well, if I have one of these every day, I can't imagine not smiling."

"I might need to give them another try then." Thornar's free hand came up under my chin, tilting my head up so I was looking up at him. "But I have a feeling that macarons aren't the reason you're blushing."

"I'm horrible at hiding my emotions," I admitted, my eyes darting to his lips. "It was that you said you loved seeing how happy they made me."

Thornar's expression turned serious, his eyes sparking. The gold in them expanded, the surge of power surrounding him reminding me just how *close* to the surface his wolf was—something my own wolf absolutely took notice of. "Your happiness means more to me than you realize, Gracie."

My eyes darted down to his lips once more as I had the bold urge to ask for a kiss. I wanted to see what his lips would taste like and how he would press his lips to mine, especially after the wave of pleasure that Basir's kiss had brought. Thornar's chest rumbled, making my toes curl as his thumb ran over my bottom lip, my skin pebbling with pleasurable shivers.

"Maybe I should taste the macarons from your lips, just to see why they make you so happy." My head spun as my stomach tightened, nervous exhilaration rushing over me.

"I would love that," I whispered. It was a bold answer, one that left my lips in honesty before I could think twice about it.

Thornar's eyes moved back down to my lips, and I could feel him move closer, anticipation rolling over me as I closed my eyes—

"Thornar!"

An unfamiliar voice shattered the moment. Thornar didn't move away, though, instead pulling back just enough so that he could turn his head. His grip on me tightened possessively. Maybe it was because I was so close to him or so keyed into him, but I could see the change overcome him.

Whoever this person was, Thornar *really* didn't like him. His entire body was tense, and his jaw was tight with frustration. No, not frustration—anger. My gaze moved from him to the individual in question.

"Esling."

Esling looked to be in his mid-thirties, and he was

wearing an Ironsun uniform, appearing to be some type of soldier. Everything about him screamed the opposite, though. The energy that surrounded him was twisted with darkness and filled with sadness. Almost immediately, his gaze moved down to me.

"I didn't realize you'd found your mate. Congratulations."

"What are you doing here tonight?" Thornar asked, pointedly not introducing the man to me. If I couldn't see his visceral anger toward the man, I would have felt insecure about why.

"Tonight? Meeting a friend. Why—am I not *allowed* to be here?" He chuckled, but the sound was off as he paled to a sickly green shade. I could practically scent the fear on him. Was he scared of Thornar? It brought to mind the conversation Tilo and Thornar had inside. Was this the man he'd been talking about?

Before I could hear Thornar's response, a sudden sharp surge of power shot through me. My body jolted, eyes squeezing shut as the bond between us flared with burning intensity.

But beneath it was something darker. Violent.

Images flashed behind my eyes: blood dripping onto cold stone, the echo of screams, a pulse of rage so sharp it made my stomach twist.

My throat tightened in panic, breath hitching as a small whimper slipped from my lips.

Then it stopped. It disappeared completely, as

quickly as it had appeared. Thornar's voice was soft and honey-dipped in my ear. "Breathe, little flame. I promise everything is okay."

My eyes were heavy, my cheeks wet with tears. I swallowed down the panic, listening as the other man's footsteps echoed in the distance.

"Was it another vision?"

I shook my head, squeezing my eyes shut to slow the pounding in my head. "No, it was different. I could feel so much anger and violence...it was overwhelming. I don't understand why I would feel that way."

My head was pressed against Thornar's chest as he held me securely against him, his arms so tight it was like he was trying to absorb me into him. I let out a puff of air, his lips brushing across the top of my head.

"I'm sorry, Gracie. I'm sorry you had to feel that."

His words were layered with something I couldn't identify, and he wouldn't let me pull back to see his expression. Instead, I stayed pressed into him until my heartbeat slowed back to normal. His energy coated me in a soft, comforting blanket, erasing everything I'd felt before. I was *safe* with Thornar.

"Who was that?" I asked, my voice tight.

"Someone we've been keeping an eye on for a while," he said, but didn't expand.

"He seemed scared of you," I murmured. "Why?"

Thornar allowed me to pull back, this time, his hands clasped on either side of my jaw. His lighthearted, easy smile was nowhere to be seen—just a seriousness that felt like cold frost drifting over my skin.

"I don't know, Gracie."

For some reason, I wasn't sure I completely believed him.

CHAPTER 21
THORNAR

I KNEW EXACTLY why Esling looked afraid—because he knew his time was up.

The Ironsun territory had a culture of modern luxury that was unique, even in Thornfell. It was something we were proud of. But there were areas that were purposefully left stained with blood from years of torture, stones that were wet with moisture, having stood on these grounds for centuries. This dungeon was one of them.

The building was an old soldier's barrack at the edge of the city, used now as a prison and place to question pieces of shit just like Esling. The mountain wind howled through the battered windows, nearly extinguishing the firelit torches. It was a bleak place— perfect for this bastard.

Still, I found myself annoyed for so many fucking

reasons, the main being that I wasn't with my little flame.

On the way back from our date, I'd immediately contacted one of our captains to ensure that neither Esling nor his point of contact went anywhere. They never stood a chance against the security measures we had throughout the city, but it was still amusing to know that both he and his point of contact had tried to run. It illuminated a lot about what their objective had been.

I'd been watching Esling for some time now because I knew he had ties to the Grimfur Skulk. We'd placed eyes throughout the city, waiting for him to mess up, and when Tilo informed me of his presence at a *fucking sweet shop*? With someone the old man didn't recognize? I knew that he'd finally made his move.

The messenger was dead, and Esling's communication had been intercepted—a note to Ivan about Gracie's presence within the Ironsun territory. Esling would die for his transaction, not only against our territory but against *my mate*. He would have put her in direct danger without a thought, her life in threat, in order to curry favor in the Cold Moon Pack. *Un-fuck-ing-acceptable.*

Which was why I hadn't let him die yet.

"You know, I should be at home, asleep with my mate," I said casually, knocking the ground with my boot as I sat on a chair facing the bastard in question. He'd already been tied up and roughened up by the guards, his right eye swollen shut and lip split. I bet he *wished* that was all he had to worry about, but I could tell how terrified he was.

Obviously, rumors about my treatment of traitors hadn't gone unnoticed.

"I didn't realize she was your mate." His voice was gargled, as if underwater. *Probably because of the blood in his mouth.*

"It shouldn't fucking matter," I growled, smiling at the way he shrank in response. "But you're right—you should have been way more fucking polite to her."

"I didn't even—"

I kicked my foot out and sent the bottom of his chair off balance, the heavy piece of furniture—and himself—collapsing onto the floor.

"What was your plan?" I asked curiously, staring up at the ceiling. "Were you planning to tuck tail and run back to Ivan? You couldn't possibly think we weren't watching you."

"I won't tell you shit."

I figured that would be the case. Standing, I rounded the bastard on the floor and put my boot on his throat, watching his face turn red with exertion. "It actually doesn't matter what you tell me. I was already planning to kill you."

A legitimate whimper left his lips.

"Do you know why?" He couldn't fucking answer, so I continued. "You *scared* her. Gracie's been scared enough. She doesn't have to feel fear anymore—not from the world, and not because of me."

I was responsible for the violence and rage Gracie had sensed through our bond. It was suppressed inside me until moments like this, and this bastard had pulled it out of me. Gracie had been forced to feel that part of me—a burden she should never have to carry—because of him.

I didn't tolerate traitors. I didn't tolerate spies. The Ironsun territory had sheltered my sister and me when we were exiled from our home, and I'd be damned if this bastard lived after trying to undermine our newfound home and, in the process, terrify *my mate*.

My mindset, my logic, may have been twisted. I could admit that. But I also didn't care—not when it came to Gracie feeling safe. I would have *never* purposefully exposed her to that side of me, and the only thing that would restore the balance was punishing this asshole for it.

"She doesn't belong here—she belongs to Ivan!"

Esling's words were his last.

The syllables hit me one by one as I pulled my gun from the holster at my hip and fired, point blank. *Once. Twice. A third time.*

Silence filled the dungeon.

I stared down at his blank, wide eyes. The holes in

the center of his skull leaked dark blood that looked black in the low lighting. And still—despite killing him—I couldn't shake the feeling that he should have suffered *more*.

"You killed him." Basir's factual tone filled the silent chamber from the doorway. "*Already*."

"He said Gracie belonged to Ivan." He shouldn't have any more questions or comments after that.

I cleared and put away my gun, walking to the far end of the room to grab a rag. Blood had splattered on me. I wouldn't normally mind, but I planned on going back to Gracie right after this.

She was safe at home with Ravik, having fallen asleep on the couch almost the minute we got back, but I needed to be close to her. I needed to know that the darkness she'd felt leaking off of me had left her— that her thoughts were far away from that.

Basir was quiet for a long moment, but I knew what he was going to say before he opened his damn mouth. We both had violent tendencies, but he was less reactive than I was. That was just the truth of it. I also knew that Esling's words would have infuriated him as much as they did me.

"You still should have waited until we were able to extract more information."

There it fucking was.

"We got everything we could out of him. Besides, he scared Gracie. She could feel my anger toward him through our bond." I hesitated. "She was terrified."

I had a feeling that something similar had happened to Basir in front of the temple—that the screams and pain she'd felt had been a reflection of him, a shadow of the emotion he kept buried.

Basir's voice was a bit sharper when he responded. "So *you* scared her."

My chuckle was dark as I turned toward him, feeling a flare of annoyance. "I would have never scared her if *he* wasn't a traitorous piece of shit."

Basir shook his head. "That's some twisted fucking logic, Thornar."

I shrugged, because he wasn't wrong—*but now I knew better.* Now I could work to keep that part of me so locked away that it didn't touch my mate, even through our bond.

"If we want to talk about twisted logic," I drawled, voice low, "let's talk about *you* dodging Gracie every chance you get—so scared to be alone with her that you end up hurting her feelings. But you're *always* watching her. Always."

"Damn right she shouldn't be alone with me," he hissed, a flash of intense panic crossing his face. "You and Ravik, of all fucking people, *know* she shouldn't be alone with me."

"No." I crossed my arms. "You're more scared of

yourself than Gracie is, and she sees right through that shit."

I was filled with rage and darkness, but I also had no problem owning that—*admitting* to it.

The silence stretched between us for a long moment before Basir deflated, shaking his head. "It doesn't matter. I couldn't stay away from her, even if I tried."

Because Gracie was absolutely everything.

"Let's get back." I nodded to the door. "We'll let the crew clean up."

The tension between us faded as we walked side by side up the stairs and out of the old barracks. It was a somewhat long walk home, and once we were under the lights of the city, the familiar sights and sounds grounding me, I felt like I could think past the cold rage I'd just experienced.

"I wonder how many more Eslings exist in the territory. I know we have eyes on a few potential spies, but something about how he acted felt...*wrong*." My voice was hushed, but Basir nodded in agreement. "He didn't panic. Or beg. Not really," I continued, frowning.

"Paired with the radio silence from the Cold Moon Pack, it just doesn't sit right," Basir agreed. "Ivan is planning something. We need to get a shadow placement on the ground to get a good gauge on what it is and how bad it is."

"I know that Deegan wants to meet Gracie tomorrow. We can suggest the move forward then. I'm sure Ravik will agree."

"Ravik was asleep when I left."

I stopped in my tracks. "He fell *asleep*? I didn't think the bastard could sleep." Obviously that wasn't completely true, but Ravik was known for being up at all hours of the night.

"Gracie." Basir's one-word answer was enough for me to understand. Gracie brought something to the three of us I hadn't even realized we needed. A softness, sure. But also a lightness that I relished in. Every hour I spent with her—the more I learned about her—the more fascinated I became.

By the time we made it back home, it was well past midnight. We entered the house silently, and without a word, I made my way toward my bedroom. Although, I didn't plan on sleeping in here often anymore. After last night, I *never* wanted to sleep away from Gracie.

A low rumble broke from my throat at that thought as I removed and stored away my weaponry, then did the same with my clothes. Sleeping in the same bed with Gracie was both paradise and a true test of my willpower. She had spent most of the night spread out on top of me, her long, silky legs intertwined with my own and her fingers gripping my chest.

I was just so fucking thankful for the oversized clothes she'd been wearing. Not that it helped how hard I was. Just her scent had done it for me, let alone the feel of her soft body tangled with mine. I knew, *I fucking knew*, that she would make the sweetest sounds when I had the chance to explore her perfection.

Not yet, though.

When I had Gracie underneath me, I wanted her to feel completely comfortable. I wanted to wring every ounce of pleasure from her body without hesitation. I knew the day would come—I felt the need our connection inspired in her through our bond—but until she was ready, I would wait.

After an ice-cold shower, trying to shake those particular thoughts of Gracie from my head, I got dressed and made my way to the bedroom. I was unsurprised to find Basir and Ravik talking quietly on the balcony, Basir likely filling Ravik in on the night's events. I didn't waste time on that, instead moving to the side of the bed that Gracie seemed to favor.

Sinking into the sheets, I pulled her toward me with an arm around her waist.

Instantly, the coldness I'd felt in my bones seeped away, replaced by a luminous warmth. My eyes grew heavy as I gave in to sleep, knowing that when I woke, I would get to do it with her in my arms.

CHAPTER 22
GRACIE

"Ravik." My voice was a soft murmur, a flush filling my cheeks at the way he was holding me. I mean truly holding me, having placed me on his lap in the center of the busy dining hall. The other two were still getting ready for the day, but the moment my stomach had made the slightest grumble we were down here, tucked into a corner, with me placed right in his lap.

Part of me felt like I should protest, but the other part of me loved it. I loved his possessive grip on my waist and the way he kept offering me food, his attention wholly on me. Instead of feeling controlling, it felt like I was being wrapped in affection. It electrified my skin and made me feel a sense of rightness.

"Yes, *lux mea*?"

"I..." I hesitated because I didn't know what to say.

I didn't want to move. "I feel like I should move," I murmured before taking another bite of muffin.

Ravik let out a low rumble of disagreement. "Why?" he asked, turning my head with a finger under my chin so I had to look him in the eye.

Motioning with my hand to the room, I just shrugged. "Everyone is looking."

"Good." Ravik's answer had a small smile tugging at my lips. "Let them look, Gracie. I'm not going to hide you away."

A small laugh nearly slipped out. "Didn't you say something about that earlier? Something about not wanting to leave bed and hiding away?"

The low, warm chuckle that left him sent shivers across my skin as he brushed his lips across my shoulder. The action made my breath catch as an image of him biting there, or on the soft part of my throat, sent desire rolling through me.

"I would love to keep you in bed, that's true." Ravik's voice was husky, making my toes curl. "But I also know I can't keep you to just the three of us. I have an entire family that's been waiting days to meet you."

"I'm excited to meet them. I just hope your dad isn't upset with me. It sounds like I derailed the trade conference for you."

"You didn't derail anything," he promised, helping me stand as I moved off his lap, eager to go meet his family now that we had talked about it. "We went for symbolic reasons. We already have trade agreements with everyone in Thornfell except the Cold Moon Pack and the Grimfur Skulk."

"Does that make it hard since they control so much of the east coast?"

He considered the question, wrapping an arm around my shoulder as we made our way out of the dining hall. "Maybe, but it's worth it. No amount of resources and trade are worth aiding the development of a damn dictatorship."

The conviction in his voice had me nodding in agreement.

"Waylon Kane from the southern region has always been open to trade as well. He's able to access most of the same products that come across the Eastern Sea."

My eyes widened. "I can't even imagine going across the sea. Traveling to Silverpine? Maybe. It's still in Iridale. But the idea of going to Florwyn, let alone anywhere past that, is insane to me."

Our world was made up of seven continents, Iridale being the one that held Thornfell and Silverpine. Florwyn was our closest neighbor over the sea to the east, made up of many small unique countries, and Goldmere was directly south of Iridale. I couldn't imagine leaving Thornfell, so the idea of visiting somewhere like that was outlandish.

"We'll fix that," Ravik promised, his tone serious. "Iridale has a rich history of shifters, but there are continents filled with other types of beings. Coralis has everything from aquatic shifters to merfolk."

I came to a hard stop as my mouth dropped open. "Like mermaids?" Of course I'd heard stories, but the idea of them being real...

"Just like mermaids."

"Wow," I breathed out. "I didn't realize..." That stab of insecurity about my lack of education rang in my ears, but Ravik was quick to soothe it.

"We'll take an afternoon and go to the library, pull some books about them," he assured me gently, his tightened grip grounding rather than overbearing. "You have forever to learn everything you want, Gracie."

And there was so much to learn.

A few moments later, we stepped through a series of heavy iron doors two floors down from the dining hall and into the brisk autumn air. I was glad I'd chosen to wear something comfortable and warm today.

I felt nervous about the impression I'd make either way, but seeing that we were meeting everyone outside made me feel better about the casual black pants and boots I'd decided to wear with a fitted gray sweater, a black coat wrapped around my frame.

"What is this place?" I asked, curiosity filling my voice.

The balcony—though it felt more like a sky court-yard—sprawled wide, perched on the roof of one of the building's upper wings. Three sides opened to the skyline, lined with glass half-walls that held back the wind but offered an unbroken view of the territory. Flags whipped in the breeze, their colors stark against the bright blue sky.

Beneath my feet, the stone floor was cool and perfectly flat, veined with lines of iron that converged in a deliberate pattern, like a path leading forward. At the far end, beneath a stretched canvas canopy, sat a full living arrangement: cushioned benches, low tables set with trays of food, even music playing softly from some hidden source. It looked like the inside of a private office had been dragged into the open air.

"This is my father's office," Ravik said, a hint of amusement coloring his tone. "He insists on doing everything outside, even in the middle of winter. Says the wind clears his head. And his wolf likes to eaves-drop on the training ground below."

The idea of his wolf eavesdropping was authenti-cally funny, but I understood why his father liked to be out here. My own wolf was jumping around playfully, trying to bite the wind.

Although, I had a feeling the embarrassing display

of excitement had more to do with Ravik's closeness to me than with being outdoors.

"Gracie!" Elowen's familiar voice had me smiling as she moved past a man I didn't recognize, who was talking with Thornar and Basir. My chest filled with happiness at just seeing them, which meant I was completely taken off guard when Elowen all but barreled into me.

"I am so, *so* glad you're okay. I didn't know what to do when you collapsed, so I'm glad we were close enough that Solenne and Isara could help."

The sudden weight of her barreling into me sent a jolt through my chest, my body tensing before I could stop it. My instincts screamed danger, but I forced a smile, not wanting anyone—let alone my new friend—to notice.

But Ravik did.

He shifted slightly to the side, not making a show of it, just...easing the pressure. His presence was a steadying force, a reminder I wasn't trapped. The subtle movement calmed the tremor running under my skin, and I realized he understood. *He always seemed to.*

Friendship mattered to me more than I could say —especially after going so long without it—and he somehow knew how to protect even that.

"I feel much better," I confirmed as she hooked

arms with me and led me forward. "It's sort of hard to explain..."

"I *totally* got the full story," she admitted. "You have a god scar on your mating bond and now Nyxarra is trying to play puppet master...or she might try that. Have we decided if we like her or not? I don't know how you feel about The Eight. My brother and I aren't really huge fans."

Elowen was a literal breath of fresh air, and the 'we' language she used about deciding how *we* felt about Nyxarra made me feel like she was taking on this situation in support of us. Wholly unnecessary, but really thoughtful. So I offered her the truth.

"Honestly, she represents so much pain from the Cold Moon Pack, so the idea of being her 'chosen' one feels...odd. I'm not sure how I feel."

"That makes sense. I wish I knew a better way to handle it or successfully ignore her. Instead I defaulted to what I know best." Elowen motioned to a massive pile of books on a table near Thornar, Basir, and the unknown man. "These are all the books I brought for you to take home! I grabbed everything I could think of from the university. You know what they say, 'knowledge is power' and all."

"Books can't protect you on the battlefield," Thornar mused, rubbing a hand up my back in greeting. Basir moved to my other side, and while he didn't touch me, I could feel his gaze on my curious expression.

Elowen brought a hand to her chest as an offended look filled her face. "*Excuse me*? Have you seen how thick they are? I could use one as a shield."

"As someone who carried all of them," the unknown man offered, "I can confirm they are very heavy and dense. Also, you would never need to use anything for a shield, so don't say that."

I stiffened, my pulse kicking up at the sudden male voice. My instinct was to take a step back, but I forced myself to stay put, even as unease prickled along my skin.

Elowen scowled at him and shook her head. "Gracie, this is Ravik's brother, Banthor."

Once she said it, it was easy to see the similarities between the two of them. He was slightly shorter than his brother but had a similar muscular build. Instead of dark hair like Ravik, though, he had honey-blonde hair that was to his shoulders. His blue eyes were completely focused on Elowen, and it drew attention to the scar that went from the bottom of his eye down to his jaw.

"Nice to meet you," I managed, my voice steady despite the nerves twisting in my stomach.

Banthor flashed me a friendly smile. "I would offer to shake your hand, but my brother or these two would probably rip it off. So good to meet you as well."

"Men," Elowen sighed, shaking her head.

I blinked, my stomach twisting. Did she actually think they'd rip off his hand? They wouldn't really do that...would they?

"*Man*—not men. There isn't a plural in your vocabulary for that." Banthor scowled, and Thornar grunted, letting out a long sigh. I looked up at him as Basir offered me a rare amused look.

"Right." Elowen rolled her eyes. "Because I only know *one* man and that's you, right?"

"Right, baby." He flashed a charming smile. "I knew you understood."

"I'm getting Sol," she grumbled, storming away.

"Your obsession over my sister is getting intense," Thornar said with a lighthearted tone that had Banthor looking over with a curious expression.

"My *love* for your sister is intense. Correct." And then he was gone.

"It has gotten somewhat funny," Basir admitted. "Especially since Banthor has been given everything in the world. So to see him struggle...it's entertaining."

"Yeah, but it's my sister, so it's uncomfortable." Thornar looked down at my confused expression. "*Mates*. Sort of," he explained. "My sister carries herself well, acting as if it doesn't faze her, but losing our parents made her hesitant. She doesn't want to lose anyone again."

"I have to assume you've just met Banthor." Ravik

rejoined us, having been sidetracked after Elowen's appearance. I nodded as he shook his head. Clearly, he knew exactly what was going on as well.

I looked over to where Elowen and Banthor were talking close to one another, her brow bent in frustration. The intensity between them made my chest tighten—was she upset? My first instinct was worry for her. Yet even through my nerves, I couldn't ignore how strangely sweet it was, the way Banthor's focus never wavered from her.

"My dad wants to meet you," Ravik said, gently leading me under the tent.

Suddenly, the idea of meeting even *more* individuals, let alone his parents, had the world pressing in around me. My chest tightened, breath catching high in my throat. The noise blurred into a dull hum, and no matter how I tried, I couldn't draw in enough air. My hands shook at my sides, heat prickling down my neck. I hadn't even realized I'd come to a complete stop until Ravik's low voice cut through the chaos.

"Gracie." A warm hand slid to the small of my back, anchoring me to the moment. "Look at me. Just me."

I forced my gaze upward, finding his golden eyes fixed on mine, calm and certain. He lowered his head until our foreheads nearly touched, his breath slow, deliberate. *"In...out,"* he murmured, guiding me with his own.

I followed—shaky at first, then steadier—clinging to the rise and fall of his chest as if it were the only tangible thing in the world. Bit by bit, the noise faded, my lungs opened, and the tremor in my hands eased.

"That's it," he whispered, his thumb brushing over my wrist. "You're safe. I've got you."

I swallowed hard, pulling back just enough to gather myself, to pretend I wasn't rattled to the core. My pulse still raced, though, and the thought struck sharp and unwelcome: *What was that?*

"I don't understand," I murmured. "I've never..."

"A panic attack," Ravik said gently, his voice steady with understanding. "That's what it was."

You'd think I would have known that feeling before now, after living on high alert, enduring so much pain. But maybe that was the difference. Maybe I'd been too focused on surviving to let myself panic.

I drew in a shaky breath and forced myself upright, grasping at composure. "We should go meet your parents." My eyes flicked to Solenne at a nearby table, her gaze already on us. She sat with two others I didn't recognize, and the reminder of more strangers waiting sent a ripple of unease through me.

We paused for a moment as we passed, Solenne reaching out to squeeze my hand.

"I'm so happy to see that you're feeling better. Isara was worried when we didn't hear an update."

"I gave one a few hours later," Ravik responded

dryly, making me smile. That clearly had not been fast enough for them.

"I think it was the next day," the man sitting with Solenne and an unfamiliar woman said. When he looked up from the game they were playing, it was obvious that he was *also* related to Ravik.

So he had at least two brothers and a sister.

"Gracie, this is Siguun, our baby brother."

Solenne's introduction nearly had a snort leaving me because the man was *huge*—as tall as Ravik, easily. He did appear younger, though. His face was slightly softer, and his short blonde hair stuck up in a few directions, making him look like he'd just woken up. The only part that didn't match was the dark, rune-like tattoos that covered his arms and ran up his neck onto his jaw. It was disarming, the contrast between that and his soft energy.

"Wonderful to meet you," Siguun said with a warm smile. He motioned to the woman across from him, her large eyes on me with interest. "This is Zia."

"I'm the best friend." She flashed a bright smile. Siguun nodded immediately. He seemed to love the label, but with the way he was looking at her, I couldn't help but think it meant more to him than that.

I could understand why. The woman had a way about her that even stood out to me. Her skin was golden, and she had long, shiny waves of hair that hung around her shoulders like silk. Her features were delicate, and her eyes had a soft tilt at the corners, giving her an expression of quiet curiosity. Despite her simple coat and the way she held herself, relaxed and non-confrontational, there was something about her that was regal in nature.

She also had a *very* different scent, her magic distinctly not wolf, but something smaller and softer. I'd been around wolves for so long that, much like the dragons at the trade conference, she stood out to me. As if knowing, her lips pulled into an understanding smile.

"Deer shifter—prey. That's why you're noticing the difference."

"Sorry, I didn't mean to make it obvious I noticed," I said immediately, feeling a wave of embarrassment.

"Don't say sorry," she assured me. "It just means you're in tune with your wolf. I enjoy being a deer shifter—I don't see it as a bad thing."

But I had the feeling others noticed, with the way she explained herself.

"You can do so many things we can't," Siguun immediately agreed. "She can run faster than me, and she can move through the forest much better—"

Zia's hand moved out to squeeze his, her cheeks flushing with color as she offered him a thankful smile. "Like I said, nothing to apologize for."

My eyes were wide because...*by The Eight, they were*

so endearing. The man may have been massive, but he was clearly a gentle giant for her.

"Mom is giving you a look, Ravik," Solenne commented, amused. I turned to see that Ravik was watching me with a soft affection.

"Come on, *lux mea*. Let's meet my father."

Malara and Deegan were sitting slightly off to the side underneath the canopy. Deegan was positioned behind his desk while Malara sat on the edge of it, talking to him. It was very obvious where Ravik and his brothers got their size from, because Alpha Deegan was large himself.

He also very clearly had Alpha power. Normally, that kind of strength made my stomach twist the way it did with Ivan—sharp and suffocating. But this...this wasn't the same. The weight of dominance was there, demanding respect, but it didn't claw at me. My wolf stirred instead, cautious yet curious, as if testing the edges of what it might mean to meet someone so powerful.

Although, there was something else I noticed as well, a thread of energy that seemed...wilted. Once again, that pull of premonition that had come in my conversation with Malara was pulled to the front. The man's laughter was bright, though, as he responded to something his wife said.

"There she is, lady of the hour—Gracie! It's wonderful to meet you!" Deegan's warm welcome surprised me, and I offered him a small smile. I'd had no idea how he was going to view me since I'd pulled his son into a direct conflict. I wouldn't have blamed him for being frustrated, even mad.

"I'm glad I'm here," I said, meeting the hand he reached out to shake. Malara gave me a warm smile in greeting. "Thank you for allowing me to stay in your territory."

"While it may not have been planned," he said, "once the boys explained the situation, I understood. After all, finding your mate—especially being *tethered* —isn't something you can ignore."

"In fact, it can drive people to do crazy things," Malara agreed, looking pointedly at him.

"I had no choice, my moon!" He barked out a laugh, explaining, "When we met back at the university, she had no idea I was the future Alpha of the territory."

"I was from Florwyn!" She scowled, crossing her arms. "I didn't know you were some future leader; I was just trying to study. I didn't have time for dating or mates."

"So instead of telling her, I followed her around for days, offering to do all of her homework and anything else to get in her good graces. It took months, but I finally got a date, and then—"

"He told me who he was." She shook her head, exasperated.

"If I'd told her from the start that I was an Alpha, she wouldn't have given me a chance." He shrugged, amused. "Have to follow the heart."

Ravik's hand tightened on my waist. Malara looked down at her husband with so much affection, I almost felt like I should look away. "It was pretty hard to ignore you. Plus, I suppose after all this time, I understand why your method worked."

"I'm so glad—" Deegan stopped, coughing hard into his elbow. Malara's softness faded away, replaced with worry. Ravik's frame was tense as he pulled me closer, almost to comfort himself. It was possible I was misreading that, but I didn't think so.

There was something wrong with Deegan; I could feel it.

"Maybe you two should grab food," Malara suggested lightly, giving her husband some water.

"Of course." Ravik led me away as Deegan continued to cough. While we made our way toward the table of food, he explained the situation in a quiet, solemn tone. "My father is sick with Moonrot. He has been for...at least five years. But it's getting worse."

"I've never heard of that," I whispered, horrified at his revelation.

"It's a cancerous disease, rotting the lungs from the inside out and only seen in wolf shifters." He breathed out. "We've tried every treatment imaginable, but nothing."

I wrapped my arms around Ravik's torso and buried my head in his chest. He tightened his around me in return, and one of his hands slid into my hair, holding me against him. I'd watched my parents die in front of me—my father's death brutal and quick, my mother's slower. But this type of disease? It brought tears to my eyes to think of the quiet grief they'd endured for years.

"I'm so sorry, Ravik," I whispered, pulling back as he cupped my jaw and examined my watery eyes. Emotion washed over his own face as he nodded, his jaw tight as if he couldn't put into words how he felt— but I could feel it through our bond.

"The old man is strong. After all the shit he's survived, I can't imagine that Astaruun is going to let this be what defeats him."

I could hear the determination and hope in his voice, and I nodded immediately. I didn't know if there was a true solution. A fix, a cure.

If there was one, I would help find it.

Was that naive of me? Possibly.

But I was starting to realize I would do a lot to help this family.

Because that's what they were. Not just a powerful pack or a group of dominant leaders—they were threaded with warmth and connection. *A true family.*

CHAPTER 23
GRACIE

"It's beautiful," I said in awe, my fingers grazing over the journal in my lap. Although to call it a journal felt inadequate. It was a piece of art.

The leather was a warm earth tone, decorated in stitches of sunset colors. Crimson, gold, and daffodil yellow were woven into whorls that reminded me of flowers in bloom, decorating the entire surface of the front, back, and spine.

A leather ribbon with my name on it was wrapped around the center of the journal, keeping the unlined, blank pieces of paper contained and safe.

My first gift in over a decade.

Ravik didn't realize how much this meant to me. I hadn't been able to read, and certainly not write, in years.

The blank pages felt like a siren song, begging me

to fill them in. To record the past, but also my new future, teeming with possibility.

"I'm glad you like it," Ravik rumbled. "I know you mentioned you don't write, but..."

"I would like to start trying," I said, squeezing his hand which rested on my leg. The garden bench we sat on was shaded by a massive pine, the privacy of the space making me feel completely at peace.

"When I was younger, I used to have a little journal. I don't even remember what I would write," I mused, my fingers running over the leather once more. "My mom loved hunting, so my brother would often join her, and when he came back, he would always have the wildest stories. I'm positive half of them were made up...but I wrote them down."

"I didn't know you had a brother," Ravik said, surprised.

"Owen," I confirmed. "He escaped during the raids. Or if he didn't, he was killed. I never saw him after that night, and I never risked asking about him. I've been thankful to have the ability to even entertain the possibility that he escaped."

Ravik's fingers came under my chin. "Do you *want* to find him?"

My eyes widened. I'd always told myself I would find him, but I hadn't ever believed it would actually happen. "That would be... Yes," I breathed out, unable to find a word to describe how it'd feel to have him back. "But I don't know how."

"We would start with a sweep and inquiry of the surrounding territories. I would just need as much info as possible on him. With a few calls to the other Alphas, I'm sure we can manage to locate him." He made it sound so simple, so matter-of-fact, as if he didn't realize that this was a *second* gift he'd be giving me.

I'd lost both of my parents, and with Owen's disappearance, my entire family. The idea of being able to find him?

I nodded adamantly, unable to find the words to express how much his offer meant.

"Then that's what we'll do," Ravik promised before offering me a hand, his warm, rough palm soothing against my own. "Now come on, *lux mea*, I want to show you around the garden." I offered him a thankful look as he tucked my journal into his coat.

"I didn't realize the garden was so large. It looked smaller from up there," I said once I'd managed to find my voice.

I'd first noticed the perfectly landscaped garden that led to a forested area during lunch. I found myself doing that often—just looking at the natural beauty of their territory—still not quite believing it was real. When I'd mentioned it, Malara and Deegan immediately suggested we go check it out at some point. Ravik had apparently decided—once Basir and Thornar mentioned having to go handle something—that 'some point' meant now.

I was excited to see the garden up close, but I was curious about what Basir and Thornar had to 'handle'.

"It's grown over time. My parents wanted a space for us to play as kids and an area of the forest that was protected. It made shifting a lot easier when we were younger. Because of my father's position, we had to be mindful of where and when we shifted."

"Because he's the Alpha?"

He nodded, his lips tugging into a smile. "Although that didn't always stop me. Thornar was worse, though, especially if he got angry."

It was hard to imagine the sunny man angry, even though I'd seen it once myself.

"I haven't shifted in over a decade." My words were meant to come off as light, more commentary than anything, but I knew they didn't as Ravik's steps came to a complete stop. The intense, controlled man turned his gaze on me, the gold burning like fire.

"Say that again."

I was suddenly uncomfortable, feeling like I'd said something I shouldn't. Something wrong. I bit down on my lip before admitting, "I haven't shifted since the raid—since I was eleven."

Ravik's stood perfectly still for a long moment, my hands tightening at my side. I knew, logically, that I wasn't in trouble, but I could feel that he was furious. It was at Ivan, I think, but it still made my heart beat rapidly.

"Give me a minute, *lux mea*," he rumbled, tugging me forward into his embrace. Despite his palpable anger, I was able to breathe out in relief the moment I was surrounded by his scent.

A long moment passed before he asked, "How is that even possible? A decade is a very long time, Gracie."

"It wasn't just me," I said softly. "Anything that connected us to our wolves was ripped away by Ivan. He didn't want anyone believing they had power or dominance. At all. Some people even claimed they stopped hearing their wolves after a few years. Mine... mine never went away, but she was silenced. At least until I met the three of you."

"Ivan Rivers can't be allowed to continue." Ravik delivered the words calmly, but they held a deep promise of violence.

"I know," I whispered, before trying to shift away from his anger. "I would like to try. I just don't even remember how."

Ravik pulled back, determination glinting in his gaze. "Come on, Gracie. We're going to try shifting."

I should have expected that. My throat tightened with nervousness and anxiety as he led me toward the edge of the forest that lined the mountain range. I could feel my wolf pacing eagerly, fascinated by the turn of events, but as I looked up at Ravik, it was clear he could see my trepidation.

"Just try. No pressure. We have all the time in the world."

Reassured and feeling safe in his presence, I looked at the lush forest in front of me. Shaking my hands out, I closed my eyes and tried to feel out my own body.

When you went so long just trying to survive, you lost grounding. When you went a decade being viewed as property, you lost the ability to feel ownership of your own body. I craved freedom, but I wasn't sure I was strong enough to take it.

I'd seen Ivan's men shift many times over the years, and something about it had always struck me as wrong. Grotesque. Their skin would burst and bones crack. Before them, I had never seen anyone shift in such a violent and painful way. It was like their wolves were fighting against them, not wanting to succumb to their will.

Visions of my parents and brother shifting played through my head as I tried to remember the sensation of shifting myself. *A warm glow in the center of my chest and the feeling of grass under my paws.* That was the strongest memory. I used to watch in awe as my mom would shift in a glow of light that wrapped around her before she appeared as a crimson wolf—beautiful but fierce. Then moments later she would shift back, her sunflower sundress absent of even a wrinkle.

That was a nifty tool of nature. Apparently, because body and clothing existed in the same 'phase' of being, when our wolves came out, it took both and would return both upon shifting back. I was glad for it because if not, there would be a lot of naked shifters everywhere.

My cheeks heated thinking about Ravik naked...

"Focus, *lux mea*." His deep rumble had me wondering if he may have felt where my thoughts had gone...which was more than a bit embarrassing.

I tried to recenter myself and focus. Of course it wasn't that easy, but the more I tried to encourage and coax my wolf out, the more I received small snippets of memories of what it was like to shift. It still wouldn't convince her to come out, though, even when I was brought to the point of pleading with her.

We can shift. No one will hurt us.

I knew that, and she knew that, but it didn't stop the panic from forming. My throat felt tight, my body acting in accordance with years of learned fear. Ivan wasn't here though. I was with Ravik, and we were safe. I just had to get my wolf on the same page.

Considering how cautious she was being, looking around for other wolves, I worried this would be a lost cause.

Opening my eyes, I looked up at Ravik, an idea

forming. "Can you...can you shift? I don't think she's going to come out unless you also shift."

I knew it was a lot to ask, yet Ravik moved back without question, a heated look in his gaze I didn't fully understand. Then in a flash—a literal bolt of lightning—he shifted into...

"You're huge!" I squeaked, my hand coming to my mouth.

When I thought back to the drug-clouded memories from the ritual, it was clear that Thornar and Basir had been gigantic as well, but since I'd been in Ravik's arms...I just hadn't realized.

Ravik moved closer, and I instinctively reached out to touch his chocolate fur as his nose brushed over my cheek. He was *that* big. Closing my eyes, I allowed myself to sink into the comfort of knowing he was right there.

My wolf was thrilled.

In fact, I'd never seen her so happy. She was sprinting through my subconscious at top speed, almost slamming into the walls of my mind. A smile tugged at my lips and I fell back, like falling into a pool of water. That was all it took for her to rush forward to greet Ravik.

Heat broke through my chest and the world exploded into an array of heightened senses. I could hear the pulse of small creatures in the forest. I could smell decay on a fallen tree to the west of me. I could taste winter in the air, carried by Sylvaern herself. I could feel mud underneath my paws, the earth wet from a recent rain. But more than anything?

When I opened my eyes, I could see Ravik. *Truly* see him, the intense power that radiated off of him and the way our bond danced with light and energy. A warm rustic brown that seemed to shimmer with gold. The other two were there as well—Basir's an onyx shade with clouds of silver smoke hanging around it, and Thornar's a pure snow white that had bursts of copper like lightning bolts. It was mesmerizing, and a soft almost purr left my throat as I moved closer to Ravik.

My gaze caught my paw as I came to a stop. *Black fur.* That was...odd. I'd always shifted into a crimson wolf like my mom. Why had that changed?

My wolf refused to consider it, though. All she wanted was to get as close to our mate as possible. I wasn't exactly in enough control to fight her, and the closer we got to Ravik, the less we wanted to ask questions and just *be*.

My nose trailed under his throat as he dipped his head, keeping me there protectively. A hum of magic rolled over both of us, and for just a moment—a fragment of time—everything felt perfect. This was my most natural state. This type of freedom was how I should *always* exist.

Suddenly, unexpectedly, I was violently pulled into darkness.

But instead of pain, I was met with *nothing* as I hit a hard surface. I gasped in pain, clutching a hand to my chest. My heart pounded so hard it felt like it might burst from my ribs, and a whimper slipped from my lips.

"Gracie Holloway."

That voice. Feminine, but layered with an ancient power that laid thick on my tongue. Chills rolled across my skin as I looked around for *her*—because I knew whose doing this was. I could feel her magic saturating the space as beams of moonlight danced in the distance.

It felt like I was staring down a long hallway into *nothingness*.

"Hello?" Any bravery I'd had while shifted retreated, fear winding tight in my chest.

"You freed me from my chains, but I am still held prisoner."

Her words hung heavy in the air as confusion clouded my mind, thickening like smoke. She told the truth, but it felt like her *own magic* was actively fighting against that declaration.

"I don't know how I freed you. I'm not sure—"

"He will use my moon to bring forth the gods in wait." Her voice fractured—infused with panic—static ringing in my ears. "He will bring forth those that wish to harm. You must—"

I was ripped away.

A kiss brought me back into reality, the demanding, hard nature of it causing me to melt as my fingers gripped onto Ravik's huge shoulders. I whimpered under the primal wave it drew from within, my wolf still so close to the surface.

My nails bit into his skin, trying to bring him closer—*needing* him to be closer. I felt like I was losing myself between fear of the unknown and overwhelming desire for Ravik.

Ripping myself away, my breathing rough and uneven, I stared up into his gorgeous golden gaze. I felt stunned, absolutely hypnotized by the man...

"What happened?" he demanded, his gaze manic.

I felt like I couldn't talk, couldn't even see, as reality began to filter back in. She'd been trying to tell me something...I just didn't understand what.

"Gracie, talk to me." His voice was a rough demand.

"I just met Nyxarra."

CHAPTER 24
GRACIE

IT SEEMED LIKE AN IMPOSSIBILITY. The book in front of me was large—one of the texts Elowen had helpfully provided—and it was completely focused on god scars. Despite its immense amount of information, somehow, it didn't mention a single thing about the physical changes that could occur because of a god scar.

Like my wolf changing fur colors.

Of course, that was fairly minor in the midst of everything that had happened—like interacting with a god—but I couldn't let it go. Neither could the three men I lived with. If not for my exhaustion and the lack of real answers, I had no doubt they'd already be pressing to uncover more about the situation I'd found myself in. Not that my wolf cared or even thought twice about it; she was moving around and offering the occasional happy *yip*, her presence vibrant in my subconscious now that we'd shifted.

I'd always imagined my wolf within my own head, moving and interacting with the world through my eyes. I hadn't realized that over time she had turned from a flash of crimson to a mere shadow, existing on the sidelines of my mind. I was beginning to understand how someone's wolf could disappear over time.

For years, my wolf had been my only constant. The thought of losing her was enough to tighten my throat and sting my eyes with grief. For the first time in longer than I could remember, I found myself thanking The Eight for something. I thanked them for keeping her with me, even after all these years without a shift.

My thoughts drifted to the last time I'd felt my paws hit the earth before the raid.

THE COOL BREEZE *rushed over me as I darted through the woods, trying to keep up with Owen. He was bigger and faster than me, but he also pushed me—and my wolf.*

When I went to school after the holiday break, I wanted to be able to keep up with the other kids during recess. I just wasn't as fast as some of them because my wolf was smaller than theirs. I couldn't count the number of times I'd wished to be taller.

A familiar howl had me pushing forward. I was almost

catching up to him—but then my vibrant red paws slid in the snowy mud, and I slammed into the ground. I immediately shifted back, scowling at the sky.

Owen's worried face appeared before me as he instantly shot out a hand to help me up. "Are you okay? I didn't even think about how slippery it is here. My bad, Gracie."

At fourteen, three years older than me, Owen had managed to get down all the cool wolf stuff that I hadn't. I was glad he was teaching me, but it still stung that I wasn't as fast or as strong.

"It's just frustrating that even when I am going fast, I can't keep my footing."

"You're getting there," he promised. "Now come on, let's get back and ask Mom to make hot chocolate."

I nodded, feeling frustrated but hopeful. Hot chocolate made almost everything better.

It was odd to consider that such a simple memory now held so much weight. Not only was it the last time I'd shifted, but the last time I'd seen Owen before the raid. Although, according to Ravik, it might not have to be. I still couldn't quite believe that.

A cool breeze came in through the bedroom window as I stood, closing the tome and making my way to the balcony doors. Shutting one side of them, I looked at the approaching storm that highlighted the mountaintops in flashes of light. I was eager to see what a storm would be like from up here, so close to the sky. A chill rolled over my recently showered skin as I made my way back to the bed and pulled the covers up over my lap.

I would just watch from under the blanket, where I could be cozy.

Small luxuries weren't things I would ever take for granted. The bath I'd taken after shifting had left my body warm and clean, my damp hair braided back against my sweatshirt-covered back. Sometimes I had flashes of life from before the raid, a similar sensation of comfort from sitting by the fireplace with my family, but the new memories were so much more intense.

It was silly to want to cry over something like a long bath, but after having nothing for so long, I couldn't feel completely weird about the urge. It didn't help that the men I lived with had gone out of their way to ensure my comfort.

Macarons sat in their ribbon-tied box on the table next to me, perfect little pastel treats I wouldn't have imagined daring to hold, *let alone eat,* less than two weeks ago. The journal from Ravik sat across the room, its pages already containing pressed wildflowers from the garden. I might not have been ready to write yet, but I could do *that.* My fingers itched to add more, especially the ones Basir had brought me after their meeting, silently placing them at the table in front of me. I felt as if keeping them safe between pieces of paper might keep the beauty of this place from fading.

I knew why I had the urge to preserve the beauty of the natural world around me—one not cursed and dead by Ivan's hand. For so long it felt as though he had tainted everything. Now I was being released from that. Even if there were things I didn't understand about my connection to Nyxarra, I was becoming confident in two important things:

One, that my bond with these men was real, something I saw evidence of with every moment I spent near them. Two, that it was going to take work to unshackle myself from the physical and mental chains Ivan had put on me.

I could only hope that it would lead to a metamorphosis—that I could become my true self.

A soft noise near the window had my gaze snapping over. A flicker of lightning caught the shape of a man in the doorway of the balcony, the shadow so still it made my breath catch. Basir's hair was mussed, shirt half undone, his eyes fixed on me with an unreadable mix of confusion and intent. For a moment, the world quieted between us before the sound of rain started against the glass.

"You're not asleep," he murmured, running a hand through his hair. There was a slight pink to the tops of his ears as I quickly put together what had happened.

The three of them had said they would stay up for

a bit, so I'd gone to shower and—they thought—fall asleep. Truthfully, I almost had. After all, the emotional weight of meeting so many people who were important to my men and of my own encounter with Nyxarra had nearly pulled me under. It had probably been about an hour, and when I still hadn't come back, he must have assumed I'd fallen asleep.

"Why didn't you just come through the door?" I asked, his damp shirt clinging to his muscles.

"I..." He paused for a long moment, leaning in the doorway. "I didn't want to wake you by opening the door."

Something about that didn't ring completely true. There were balconies that ran along the outside of our suites, so I assumed he'd scaled them.

"Do you do that often?" I asked softly, standing and approaching him. His jaw tightened. I had a feeling I was close to hitting the mark, but there was something here I didn't fully understand.

"Do I come into your room while you're sleeping?" he demanded roughly, his emerald eyes so dark they almost appeared black. His posture was relaxed, but I could feel how tense my question made him, and I felt a tinge of nervousness. I didn't want to upset Basir, but I also felt the urge to tear down the walls between us—to better understand what was going on in his head.

"Yes."

After a long moment, he nodded sharply, a heat to his gaze that caused my chest to flutter. He seemed hesitant about my reaction, almost worried I would be mad. I didn't understand it at all.

"I don't mind," I whispered, realizing why the concept was more appealing than I would have expected. "The idea of you watching me makes me feel safe."

A low rumble caught in Basir's throat as he tightened his hands at his sides, as if he were holding back physically. I went a step further. "But I would rather you just stay, then. Thornar and Ravik have slept in here...you should, too."

I hadn't meant it to sound so forward—so blunt—but my words had an instant effect.

Basir moved into my space, just like that first night, in a flash—like a shadow himself. I inhaled sharply as his fingers ran over my throat and into my hair, holding me in place as he dipped his head down, brushing his nose against mine. I shivered at the intensity of his movement, my heart beating wildly, wanting more of his touch. Somehow, the man was managing to hold me close while keeping me at a distance.

"I can't be in your bed, glow," he said in a soft, pained whisper. My eyes grew heavy at the unexpected grief in his voice.

"Why?"

"I just...I can't." He grit the words out and then forced himself to add, "Ever."

Ever? My brows pulled together as pain filled my heart. I tried to pull back, but he kept me against him as he continued, soft and almost threatening. "You don't realize what you're asking for when you say that."

Maybe he was right...

No. He wasn't, and his implication made me angry. Pulling away, I stepped back, and something about my expression had him looking tormented himself.

"I may not know a lot, Basir, but I know I want you close."

"Gracie, I *can't* be close to you," he hissed, his fists tightening at his sides. "I can't hold you like Ravik or Thornar do. I can't be soft with you—I don't have the ability."

"You have before," I argued. He was erecting a gigantic wall between us, bigger and more daunting than ever before.

He moved a hand through his hair in frustration, my gaze catching on his tattoos, the inky shapes lined with gold. Knowing Basir as I did now, I could see how much they reflected him—a shadow with a vibrance inside that he tried to hide. But I didn't want him to hide from me.

"Barely," he whispered, more to himself than to me.

I could practically feel the pain through our bond, and I felt the confusion and the guilt. He didn't feel good about what he was saying, but he felt like he had to say it. I never wanted him to feel forced to do anything; I'd felt that enough in my life.

Maybe I needed to first figure out why he felt that way.

"Can you tell me why?" I asked softly. It was hard to get the question out—I wasn't used to the idea of being able to ask, let alone demand an answer. His gaze immediately sharpened on mine. He took a moment to examine my expression, then shook his head.

I tried to hide my disappointment, but then he explained.

"I was born in the Grimfur Skulk territory."

Oh. That was the one territory I actually knew. I'd heard Ivan complain about it at dinner often, whenever he had to visit. The streets were paved with stone and dirt, the air hung with a heavy industrial smog, and the territory itself was violent—filled with predators that acted freely, unlike the harsh structure of the Cold Moon Pack.

Both places were filled with evil, but in different ways.

Basir looked out at the balcony in thought, away from my wide-eyed expression, his voice so low that I had to move closer to hear. "My parents worked and died as shockdust runners. I don't think I had been part of the plan, but once I was old enough, I became part of their ventures."

Shockdust. I'd heard Ivan's men talk about it before. Apparently it could keep someone up for days on end, a stimulant made specifically for soldiers. So Basir's parents had been drug runners, and he'd been forced to be one as well.

"Basir..."

"It was a dangerous life. I was abducted to pay debts more times than I can count, and I was sold off by them at least twice. It wasn't until I was old enough and big enough to hold my own that I could stop that shit. At that point, though, I was completely embedded in the system. I was running shockdust right alongside them."

It was the most I'd heard Basir say at once, and I was captivated.

"The Grimfur Skulk's drug trade is expansive. They provide more for Thornfell than any other territory. The market is drenched with blood. I didn't even realize how light the world could be outside of those walls..." His gaze went distant as he ran a hand over the tattoos that stretched down his arm. "My parents were killed when I was ten, during a conflict between city factions. I managed to escape. I fled the territory because their competition wanted me dead as well."

"That is *horrible*," I whispered, stepping closer to

him. He tensed slightly but didn't move back. His hand darted out to rest on my waist as he finally met my gaze, the sadness there seeping into my very bones. "No one should be forced into that, especially so young."

Basir nodded as if he knew that, but it didn't seem to sink in. "Until I left, my world was bathed in darkness. It was only after I broke free that I saw that light even existed, Gracie. The darkness isn't gone. It will never be gone."

I heard his declaration, but I didn't fully understand. Why would that stop him from wanting to be near me? To be in my room? Did he think he couldn't be happy—couldn't enjoy our closeness? Or maybe he was saying that because of the darkness, he didn't feel what the others did...

"Does the bond feel different to you because of that? Do you not feel the same—"

Basir shook his head emphatically, stopping me in my tracks. "How I feel about you, glow, is only intensified by the darkness. That's the problem."

I wasn't sure I fully understood, yet I treated his words as a sign of his emotions and chose courage in the face of it.

"Just because you've lived in darkness doesn't mean you can't enjoy the light."

My statement seemed to cause Basir immense

pain, his eyes closing as he stood perfectly still for a long time. *Had I said something wrong?*

When his eyes opened again, I could see vibrant green streaks within the emerald. Without a word, the man lifted me up and carried me toward the bed. I watched as he gently laid me on it and went to dim the lights. I held my breath, not wanting to ruin the moment.

Finally, as he returned, my curiosity won out.

"Are you joining me?" I asked, my voice filled with a soft need I could hear myself.

Basir moved into the bed, adjusting my frame so I melted against him, his heartbeat steady and solid beneath my cheek. He brushed his lips over the top of my head.

"Basir?" I needed something from him. "What are you doing?"

His chest produced a low rumble, his gunpowder and sandalwood scent wrapping around me, as he admitted, "Just basking in the light, glow."

CHAPTER 25
BASIR

TWENTY-TWO MINUTES. I lasted twenty-two minutes before I had to force myself from her bed, retreating to the shadows where I could watch her safely. My gaze traced over her peaceful expression as lightning from the storm outside filled the room with momentary silver before submerging me back into darkness.

It was hard to put into words, especially to Gracie, how deep the dark well of my soul was. How the petroleum scent of shockdust in back alleys and the feel of slick blood on cobblestone had become a part of me. How I existed as an ink stain on a beautiful piece of paper. How I lived as a shadow to my *own* life.

I savored the light, but I would never own it. I'd killed far too many for that to be possible. I had marked my skin with shadows and light to remind myself that while there was a vibrancy to life, it would never be mine to hold.

Just like Gracie.

She would always be out of reach, her perfection like a glowing sunset slipping through my blood-stained fingers. My glow breathed perfection, and she existed as a pinnacle of light and beauty.

Which was why I needed to stay the fuck away from her.

I would ruin her, like everything else I'd touched. The darkness and depravity that twisted inside of me tried to latch onto her whenever she was within reach, selfishly wanting to absorb her lightness, to bathe in it while dragging her down into the darkness so she couldn't escape.

Gracie didn't realize that I was a threat to the freedom she so tentatively held. If I gave in, I would shackle her to me. I couldn't love her any other way.

And what I wanted from her physically...I shook my head at that thought. Her kiss and touch were so sweet, so much so that it was painful, and the way she looked up at me was filled with trust that surged through our bond. But if she knew how I wanted to own every inch of her, to demand she give me every-thing so there were no parts left untouched, she would be terrified.

She would look at me like the monster I was.

No. I could never take her as mine. Gracie had just

escaped a master, and I wouldn't become her new jailer.

It didn't remove my desperate need for her, though.

A low rumble broke from my throat as my gaze lingered over her body. One leg was over the sheet, her body curled on her side, her sweatshirt pushed up at her hip to reveal a pair of sleep shorts. She slept without regard to her safety, completely trusting me. And I was actively betraying that trust, imagining all the ways I could ruin her.

I wanted to hear her soft, sleepy moans as she melted under my touch, my tongue tracing her skin as she lay open and vulnerable to me. I wanted to feel how she would squeeze around me as I slid slowly into her tight heat, having teased her until she was soaking wet, infiltrating her dreams with my mere touch. I wanted to watch her come around me as I stroked in and out of her, her body trembling as I spilled inside her, marking Gracie *completely*.

I wanted to be able to leave my mark inside her, to bring her pleasure without her ever seeing the darkness inside of me—something I wouldn't be able to hide from her unless she was like *this*. Completely mine yet safe...from me.

Ripping my gaze away, I let out a harsh breath and ran a hand over my face. I needed to get out of here. I would never be worthy of my glow.

But no matter where I was, I would crave Gracie obsessively. I would take any touch she willingly gave, even if it was agonizing how badly I wanted her.

I was a fucking addict for any attention she would give me.

I went to leave, to repress the need ringing in my head, but before I could, a glow emanating from the bed had me moving closer in confusion. As if The Eight were mocking me, I watched as Gracie's soft skin shimmered with an otherworldly glow.

It wasn't light—it was pure temptation, spilling over her skin in delicate, molten gold. My fingers moved before my mind could stop them, tracing the shimmer.

It vanished at my touch.

It was a gut punch that nearly made my knees buckle as anger, sadness, and frustration fought within me. What was wrong with me? Putting my head down, I forced myself to step back, feeling shaken to my core and knowing that I needed to leave. Now.

"Basir?" Gracie's voice was sleepy, and I felt guilty for waking her as I slowly looked up, finding her watching me with sadness.

"I have to leave." My voice was harsh, causing her to blink as she sat up, confused.

"I don't want you to. I want you to stay."

I wished I could have controlled myself, but I

didn't have the willpower anymore. I moved forward in a fast, predatory movement, pinning her to the bed. My lips slammed against hers, and a moan left her lips as her fingers slid into my hair. The slight tug had my cock hardening as I pressed down on her, feeling her body open for me, her legs falling to either side of my hips.

Our kiss was heated and desperate, the need between us slashing at our bond and demanding attention—demanding we give it what both of us so clearly wanted. Her soft vanilla and cinnamon scent filled my lungs, and I broke away for only a singular moment as I brushed my lips down her jaw to graze her throat.

I could imagine my teeth slicing into her skin, marking her as mine. I could feel how wet and hot she was through her sleep shorts, and I could picture the feeling of her clutching around me before coming. *Fuck.* I let out a low rumble as my hand moved to her waist, slipping underneath her sweatshirt, wanting to touch her, wanting to feel more of her—

Scarred skin met my fingertips.

My breath stalled, and my brutal world narrowed to that patch of roughened flesh. Rage, bright and blinding in its heat and power, exploded inside of me. My vision filled with red as I sat back just enough to push her sweatshirt up, a concerned noise leaving her throat. A deep, primal growl left my chest at the vision that greeted me.

Puckered, rough skin covered the left side of her torso, as far up as I could see and down to her hip—and I knew that the scarred tissue was only a flicker of the agony she'd suffered from the burn that caused it.

"Who did this to you?" My voice was raw and broken.

Her body trembled as fear infused our bond. I couldn't... I couldn't fix that, not until I knew who'd hurt her—who had caused her so much torment, so much pain.

Gracie squirmed underneath me, and when I pulled back from her she tucked her legs against her chest, her sweatshirt falling to cover her. A vulnerable expression was painted on her face as she looked at me with slight fear but also embarrassment. I didn't have the words to express how much fury was coursing through me, but I knew my reaction was upsetting her —hurting her.

My fingers moved to graze her jaw as I spoke in a harsh voice. "Answer me."

Her gold eyes fell shut as she let out a heavy exhale. "The night of the raid, when I was taken from my home, one of Ivan's men used my body to open a door that was alight with flames. I know it's hideous."

I could see her shame, the way she wouldn't meet

my gaze. Suddenly, my rage was incomparable to my need to comfort her. *I would kill whoever did this.* That wasn't in question. But in this moment, Gracie was far more important than revenge.

Gracie fell back on the bed as I moved forward and held myself over her, brushing my nose against hers. My voice portrayed every ounce of the emotion I felt, and some I hadn't even realized would leak through. "There isn't an inch of you that could ever be considered hideous, Gracie. That scar shows what you survived. It shows how you healed despite your imprisonment."

A small sniff had me pulling back as I realized that tears were welling in her eyes. She stared at me with a warm thread of affection that radiated through our bond.

Gracie's response was soft, almost a whisper, but it shot straight through my heart. "Couldn't I say the same about your darkness?"

The anger seeped out of me as I stared down at her, my own history trying to claw up my throat. I found myself speechless in the face of her ability to pinpoint exactly where I stood.

"No," I said, forcing the truth to leave my lips. "*You* are a survivor. You were a victim of cruelty. I inflicted it." It was as clear as I could make it.

"Did you? Or did you defend yourself from the life you were placed in, the cards you were dealt? Inflicting violence in reaction to a dangerous situation is not the same as being cruel or bad, Basir. You were ten."

She was clawing at those doors I kept sealed, the vault I kept buried. I couldn't...I wouldn't let myself think that she could be right. I *could* comfort her, though. Or at least try to.

I dipped my head down and kissed her soft lips gently, not allowing myself more, before pulling back. I saw the disappointment at the wall I was putting up between us, but she had to know—she had to understand—that it was to protect her.

"I didn't mean..."

I moved next to her in bed as she stared at me with concern. I immediately brought her against me, giving in to the moment because I wasn't strong enough to convince her to see me for the monster I truly was. Not tonight—not feeling this emotionally raw.

"If you want me here, I'll stay tonight."

She graced me with a beautiful smile, as if I was worthy of that light.

I hadn't given her what she truly wanted—belief that I could be salvaged—but if she wanted to rest her head against my chest, to allow me the pleasure of holding her, I wouldn't fight it. Not in the darkness of this room. Not while my shadows pulled at me and she glowed in my arms like a sunset I could never quite reach.

I would watch over her with permission. And

tomorrow, in the brilliant light of day, I would do better. I would protect her better—even, and especially, from myself.

CHAPTER 26
GRACIE

"You look beautiful, little flame."

My cheeks heated as Thornar appeared in the doorway of the bathroom where I was finishing getting ready. I'd put on a hunter-green wool skirt that tightened at the waist and went out to my ankles, a pair of black boots and socks cradling my feet. It was particularly cold out, so I'd even put on a black turtleneck to go with it. It wasn't a fashionable outfit by any means, so his compliment gave me a sense of pride.

"Thank you," I said sincerely as I finished brushing my hair out before clipping back the top half. I could see the change in my health physically manifesting in how I appeared. My skin had a pinkish glow, and my hair felt silkier than it had in years. Even my eyes had a warm glow to them, the dark circles having completely disappeared. "I promise I'm almost ready."

"Take your time," he insisted. "I'm more than happy to just watch you for hours."

My cheeks burned brighter as I turned and stepped toward him. "I have a feeling that might be a bit boring," I teased. When his arm hooked around me, I melted against his chest like I'd been doing it for years.

"Never." He smoothed a hand up my throat to hold my jaw. "I'm fascinated by you, Gracie." A string of excitement and pleasure crashed over me at his simple statement.

It was almost impossible to imagine that a man like Thornar found me interesting, let alone that he was *fascinated* by me.

"That seems unthinkable to me," I whispered. "I don't do anything interesting."

"*You.* You are interesting, not what you do," he murmured. There was a glint to his gaze that told me he was ready for battle—that if I didn't believe him, he would point out all the reasons why.

"Okay," I whispered, smiling. "I won't try to talk you out of wanting to pay attention to me."

That may have sounded more pathetic than I had intended.

He let out a low rumble. "Good girl."

Without any warning, the man dipped his head and slid his lips against mine. I let out a surprised sound but immediately gave in to his dominant hold. The way he kissed was both teasing and in control, as if he had all the time in the world. He tugged at my bottom lip before his tongue soothed over the sting, causing a whimper to slip from my lips. I felt light-headed, almost high, by the time he pulled back, my legs almost shaky from the pull the man had on me.

"Wow," I whispered as he chuckled, the warm sound curling around me as I stared at him in awe.

"I'll take that, little flame." He winked. "Come on, let's get you some food before we leave." I followed him out of the room, still feeling dazed by the kiss as he intertwined our fingers, brushing his lips over the top of my hand.

It was late morning, the sunshine casting the main room in a bright glow. Ravik was eating breakfast next to a plate clearly meant for me as Thornar pulled out my chair and motioned for me to sit.

"Where's Basir?" I asked. Ravik looked up from the papers in front of him and smoothed a hand over my leg in greeting.

"Getting ready. Before we go anywhere for the day, we need to go to that meeting," Ravik explained as Thornar went to make coffee. The scene was domestic in a way I had never experienced before, and it caught me off guard by how much I loved it.

"You don't have to go to the meeting," Thornar reminded me. "Only if you want to."

"I do," I promised.

When I'd woken to Basir still in bed with me, I'd

been thrilled. Last night had been intensely emotional, and in the light of day, I worried he'd pull back. I think he'd tried to, but instead had spent at least fifteen minutes with an arm wrapped around me, his lips brushing over my forehead again and again. When we finally got up, he explained that we needed to go over not only what I'd seen in my vision yesterday but also new intel from the Cold Moon Pack.

I *very* much wanted to know what Ivan was doing since the failure of his ritual. It was both a terrifying and necessary piece of information for the puzzle of my future.

"I also have a lead on your brother."

My eyes widened as I put down the fork I'd been lifting to my mouth. Ravik gave me a knowing look as he tapped the plate. I brought it back up to my mouth, urging him to continue.

"I contacted Kaliyah Greene, the one who just hosted the trade council," he started, and I nodded in understanding. "As well as Waylon Kane. Their territories border the Grimfur Skulk, which Owen would have presumably had to pass through on his way out."

"Or he could have gone north to Silverpine," Thornar pointed out.

Ravik nodded. "I did check with them, but they haven't gotten back to me yet. Although they may not need to now. Eight years ago, an Owen Holloway— mid-teens—was recorded passing into the Scarlet

Sloth territory by border patrol. I haven't managed to track him past that, but it looks like...

"Gracie?"

A small sob almost bubbled out of my mouth. I put my hand over it, my fork clattering to the plate. Relief like I'd never experienced overwhelmed me as tears leaked down my face.

"Shit," Thornar cursed, moving around the island and smoothing a hand up my back.

Ravik's hand tipped up my jaw as I looked right at him, not trying to hide my tears. "I *really* thought he was dead, Ravik. I thought they'd killed him that night."

Thornar nodded, not saying anything, and Ravik's gaze filled with understanding. "We'll find him, Gracie. I promise."

"Why the fuck is she crying?"

Basir's voice almost made me jump. He appeared across the island looking panicked, his harsh tone instantly making me worried. Neither of the other men seemed bothered by his reaction in the least, though, as I offered him a watery smile.

"We found a lead on my brother. Good tears."

Basir grunted, running a hand through his hair. "Rarely are tears good, glow. Rarely."

I truly believed he meant that.

"Alright," Thornar said. "Well, before Basir decides to kill us for making you cry, let's get on to this meeting. We'll keep moving our search forward for Owen. Don't worry, little flame. It's our top priority to find your brother."

"Thank you," I whispered, feeling so grateful for these men.

As we made our way to the private meeting room one floor down, the men quietly explained what they'd been doing to monitor Ivan and what they'd found. At first I was overwhelmed by the amount of information, but when I'd asked to be part of the meeting, they had taken that as a sign I wanted to be informed about everything. It was unexpected, given how women were treated in the Cold Moon Pack—their opinions or involvement in anything outside of domestic work was minimal—but it meant so much to me. It made me feel valued in a way I had never felt before.

"We figured Ivan would be reactionary to what happened," Ravik said, "but instead he went silent, so we sent in a shadow patrol to monitor and gather intel."

"What's a shadow patrol?" I asked.

"They're a special operations squadron. They focus on infiltration and information gathering," Basir explained.

"Basir was part of one for a bit," Thornar added casually. Basir shot him a frustrated look that I didn't understand.

"They managed to return with...a lot. Not all of it fits together in a picture, but maybe you'll be able to get a better grasp on it than us." Ravik rubbed his hand across my back.

"They've doubled the presence at their borders, and supplies have been moving in and out of North-grove, some from the Grimfur Skulk territory," Basir said, his brow dipping. "He's planning something."

With Ivan, that was never a good thing.

We stepped inside the meeting room, greeted by familiar faces. The room itself was windowless, maybe the size of the bedroom I'd been sleeping in, and held a large circular table cluttered with artifacts and paperwork.

Two uniformed soldiers stood at attention against the wall behind Alpha Deegan. His gaze was on the papers in front of him, and Malara spoke quietly to Elowen. It was interesting who was gathered, and I had a feeling it was purposefully kept very small—filled with only essential people. Including two that I was surprised to see.

Isara and Solenne stood off to the side, seemingly debating something. I was surprised they were here until I remembered what I'd read about the priests and priestesses in the territory. Each was trained in both medical care and combat, for when—or if—they ever had to be on the field. I hadn't found proof that it happened often, but it did clarify why they were here outside of their knowledge of the gods.

"Morning!" Elowen said. I offered her a small smile as Alpha Deegan got started.

"Let's jump right into it. We'll have to hold a meeting to brief the captains later, but I wanted all of us on the same page first," he said as we sat down. In front of each chair was a stack of papers—intel reports.

"They're obviously planning something," Thornar said.

"It's not an attack," Malara stated as she watched Isara and Solenne finally join us.

"No," Solenne agreed.

"And their troop movement appears to be focused on defense," Thornar pointed out.

"So they assume *we* will attack soon?" Elowen frowned. "I've spent the past two days studying Ivan and his normal patterns, and that doesn't really fall in line. He's very reactionary."

My gaze moved over the objects on the table— things I assumed were gathered from the compound. A Nyxarra-marked relic and ceremonial banners decorated with a red moon lay scattered among a series of bottles, each filled with different herbs.

"Where did all of this come from?" I waved my hand toward the items.

"One of the smaller shipments we intercepted,"

Isara explained. "We were just talking about how it looks like ritualistic elements."

"He performs rituals monthly," Ravik stated, looking down at me. I nodded. That alone wasn't odd, but my gut was telling me I was missing something.

"He also appears to be moving people around," Deegan said, pulling out a piece of paper. "He's repopulating the Northgrove compound—almost triple its normal amount."

"*Triple?*" I pulled out the paper to see it for myself. On it were photos of trucks coming and going, all filled with terrified faces. "Never once in the past decade has he moved that many people to a compound. At least not the one I was at."

My head began to pulse as they started to throw around ideas. Closing my eyes, I was hit with a wave of nausea as something tried to break through my consciousness. A cool wind rushed over my skin and smoke wrapped around me, cloaking me in darkness. I groaned, feeling my world twist and turn in a familiar sensation.

Nyxarra. This was her doing.

I didn't land anywhere this time; instead, I floated as the world around me began to flash with images I didn't understand. At least, not at first.

Thousands of faces were turned upward, their gazes feverish, skin painted with Nyxarra's sigils.

Above them, the full moon burned a deep, bloody

crimson, its light staining the ground as if the earth itself bled.

Ivan stood at the heart of it all, framed in the shadow of a towering beast whose roar shattered the air.

My eyes snapped open as the vision broke. I gasped, a hand coming up to my throat as the taste of blood filled my mouth. Everyone was staring at me in shock, and for just a moment, I wondered if I would pass out. My eyes fell heavy as I heard the softest whisper in my head:

"A sacrifice to open the gates."

"Gracie." Thornar's voice grounded me, my bond thrumming with concern and panic over my state. I needed to say something.

"A vision," I whispered. "Of a sacrifice. Of thousands, underneath the next full moon."

Eight days had passed since the previous ritual...

"The Hunter's Moon." Elowen floated the name softly. My stomach dropped.

"I don't understand," Solenne said in shock. "Are you saying that his reaction to this previous ritual being interrupted is to do a ritual sacrifice of *thousands*?"

"A madman," Isara whispered, horrified.

"Yes...I think that's exactly what he's doing. He's going to sacrifice all of them to Nyxarra."

"But she wouldn't want that!" Elowen squeaked. "Surely she's told you that."

"She must be showing you his plan for a reason," Ravik agreed.

"I don't know," I said. "I really don't know. His rituals have never helped our territory before, so I'm not sure why he'd think this time would be different."

Deegan and Malara exchanged a long look before Deegan offered, "Is it possible the rituals weren't meant for the land, but for him? For his own power?"

Oh. Ivan was always right at the altar, taking in every moment of the rituals...but Nyxarra clearly didn't want this. So why would she give him her blessing?

"What if Nyxarra isn't the one making him more powerful?" I asked, testing the idea. "What if the vision I saw of her being imprisoned is because she's being forced to serve Ivan? I don't know if that's possible, but she clearly doesn't want *this* to happen."

My words weighed heavily in the room as each of us considered what it would take to force a god's hand like that. I needed all of the pieces to the puzzle, but it felt like they'd been thrown across all of Thornfell.

"It can't happen," Basir said, his tone final. "We have *twenty days* if he plans to do this on a full moon."

"Before he brutalizes everyone in his damn territory," Thornar rumbled.

Ravik's gaze locked on mine, his voice low and certain. "If he completes this ceremony..." He hesitated, letting the silence stretch, every eye in the room fixed on him.

"Ivan Rivers will be a god of this world."

*HOWLING **Desire*** is available for order today!

ON THE FOLLOWING PAGE, *you'll find* **The Thornfell Registry:** Territories & Command and Genealogy & Relations.

THE **HUNTER'S Moon Ritual** Series:

- Howling Love
- Howling Desire
- Howling Fate

THE THORNFELL REGISTRY

TERRITORIES & COMMAND

- The Cold Moon Pack Territory
  - Alpha: Ivan Rivers
- The Ironsun Pack Territory
  - Alpha: Deegan Gentry
- The Scarlet Sloth Territory
  - Alpha: Kaliyah Greene
- The Grimfur Skulk Territory
  - Alpha: Graeme Sharp
- The Stark Flight Territory
  - Alpha: Waylon Kane
- The Bloodrose Sloth Territory
  - Alpha: Lacey Harrison

- The Nightstar Flight Territory
  - Alpha: Haiden Murphy
- The Blazefur Pride Territory
  - Alpha: Chace Wall

GENEALOGY & RELATIONS

- **The Holloway Family**
  - Cal Holloway
  - June Holloway
  - Owen Holloway
  - Gracie Holloway
- **The Gentry Family**
  - Deegan Gentry
  - Malara Gentry
  - Ravik Gentry
  - Banthor Gentry
  - Solenne Gentry
  - Siguun Gentry
- **The Veydran Family**
  - Dane Veydran
  - Anwen Veydran
  - Thornar Veydran
  - Elowen Veydran
- **The Morcant Family**

- [NAME REDACTED]
- [NAME REDACTED]
- Basir Morcant

M. SINCLAIR

M. Sinclair is a USA Today Best-Selling Author who can be found writing or thinking about her characters and plots nearly every moment of the day. With over 65 published works since her debut in 2019, her work spans from paranormal to contemporary romance rooted in extensive world-building and deep character development. M. Sinclair believes there is enough room for all types of heroines in this world, and that being saved is just as important as saving others.

Just remember to love cats... that's not negotiable.

PUBLISHED WORKS

M. Sinclair has crafted different universes with unique plotlines, character cameos, and shared universe events. As a reader, this means that you may see your favorite character or characters... appear in multiple books besides their own storyline.

UNIVERSE 1

Established in 2019

VENGEANCE

Book 1 - Savages

Book 2 - Lunatics

Book 3 - Monsters

Book 4 - Psychos

Complete Series

Vengeance : The Complete Series

THE RED MASQUES

Book 1 - Raven Blood

Book 2 - Ashes & Bones

Book 3 - Shadow Glass

Book 4 - Fire & Smoke

Book 5 - Dark King

Complete Series

A Raven Masques Novel - Birth of a Raven

Red Masques: Volume One

Red Masques: Volume Two

TEARS OF THE SIREN

Book 1 - Horror of Your Heart

Book 2 - Broken House

Book 3 - Neon Drops

Book 4 - Snapped Strings

Book 5 - Fractured Souls

Book 6 - Shattered Galaxies

Complete Series

DESCENDANT

Book 1 - Descendant of Chaos

Book 2 - Descendant of Blood

Book 3 - Descendant of Sin

Book 4 - Descendant of Glory

Book 5 - Descendant of Pain

Book 6 - Descendant of Victory

Complete Series

UNIVERSE 2

Established in 2020

AMONG SHADOWS

Book 1 - Court of Betrayal

Book 2 - Court of Deception (TBA)

PARANORMAL & FANTASY SERIES

THESE SERIES ARE NOT CURRENTLY AFFILIATED WITH A SPECIFIC M. SINCLAIR UNIVERSE.

HUNTER'S MOON RITUAL

Book 1 - Howling Love

Book 2 - Howling Desire

Book 3 - Howling Fate

PHASES OF THE MOON

Book 1 - Lunar Witch

Book 2 - Blood Witch

Book 3 - Shadow Witch

Book 4 - Unblessed Witch

Complete Series

The Storm Dragons' Mate

Book 1 - Blitz

Book 2 - Flicker

Book 3 - Surge

Book 4 - Flash

Complete Series

The Dead and the Not So Dead

Book 1 - Queen of the Dead

Book 2 - Team Time with the Dead

Book 3 - Dying for the Dead

Complete Series

The Dead and the Not So Dead: Completed Series

Silver Falls University

Book 1 - Lost

Book 2 - Forgotten

Book 3 - Discovered

Book 4 - Pursued

Book 5 - Found

Complete Series

I.S.S.

Book 1 - Soothing Nightmares

Book 2 - Defending Nightmares

Book 3 - Defeating Nightmares

Book 4 - Loving Nightmares

Universe Standalone Novel - Mating Monsters

Complete Series

CONTEMPORARY UNIVERSE

Established in 2021

THE SHADOWS OF WILDBERRY LANE

Book 1 - Perfection of Suffering

Book 2 - Execution of Anguish

Book 3 - Carnage of Misery

Complete Series

Complete Collection: The Shadows of Wildberry Lane

THEIR POSSESSION

Book 1 - Sheltered

Book 2 - Searched (TBA)

Book 1 - Wings of Stars

Book 2 - Wings of Pain

Book 3 - Wings of Hope (TBA)

The Vampyres' Source

(M. Sinclair & R.L. Caulder)

Book 1 - Ruthless Blood

Book 2 - Ruthless War

Book 3 - Ruthless Love

Complete Series

Rebel Hearts Heists Duet

(M. Sinclair & Melissa Adams)

Book 1 - Steal Me

Book 2 - Keep Me

Complete Duet